Oceans Apart

by

L B Baxter

Copyright © L B Baxter, 2015

The right of L B Baxter to be identified as the author of this work has been asserted by her in accordance with the Copyright, Designs and Patents Act 1988.

All rights reserved. No part of this publication may be reproduced, stored in a retrieval system or transmitted in any form or by any means (electronic, mechanical, photocopying, recording or otherwise), without the prior written permission of the author.

Editorial & Design Services: The Write Factor
www.thewritefactor.co.uk

'Every moment I shape my destiny with a chisel, I am a carpenter of my own soul.'
– Rumi

Contents

1	A dangerous question	1
2	A long way down	8
3	Jura meets her menfish	16
4	A bit of common courtesy	24
5	Shell, shock	35
6	Seven suggestions for serenity in the sea	47
7	The rule of opposites	57
8	A decision of some urgency	70
9	Octalma, Octrus and the octopi	84
10	A matter of choice	98
11	A golden truth	116

CHAPTER 1

A dangerous question

In the depths of an ocean far away from some and a little closer to others, millions of fish lived side by side. Two thick-scaled fish, who insisted on being called the King and Queen, watched over them to ensure they obeyed the rules. The King and Queen were predators who took pleasure in terrorizing the fish night and day and the fish remained obedient and docile, not because they respected the King and Queen, but because they feared them and never thought it possible to question the way in which they were being told to live.

Life at the bottom of the sea really wasn't much fun at all. In fact, each and every fish that lived there was miserable, although most did not realize it. They accepted that there was no alternative so they had better just get on with it. There was never enough food for them all on the seabed so life was very stressful and it was always a struggle to meet their basic needs. Huge fights would break out over one morsel of algae and inevitably the most aggressive would always win. The most important rule of all was one that was so well-known to the fish it was almost as if it had been implanted at birth: They were not permitted, under any circumstances, to swim higher than 10ft above the seabed. The thought of venturing further up was terrifying so they preferred not to even think about it, let alone mention it. It was because of this that none of them knew why they weren't allowed to go there. They would never dare ask, for asking would be acknowledging the existence of a place higher than where they lived and this, of course, was out of the question.

    The fish were expected to learn the ways of their world immediately. If, after a matter of days, they were not behaving in a way that was expected of them, they would be locked away until the King and Queen were satisfied they had learnt their lesson and would no longer be an embarrassment to the shoal. There were no schools or teachers to help them learn this knowledge, they were just supposed to know, so it really was very difficult for them. Some fish seemed to know everything automatically but the ones that didn't were terrified of having to admit they did not know something. These fish were called stupid and once you had been labelled as such, your tail was torn. In fact, your tail was torn if the King or Queen decided you were not fit to own your tail and that could be for any reason, depending on their mood.

The torn-tails had the hardest time of all, for once a torn-tail, always a torn-tail. Mixing with one would be like admitting that you were stupid too. They were ostracized from the shoal and although many fish pitied them, some were quite pleased to have someone to look down on. It gave them a sense of importance, a feeling that, however bad things got, at least they weren't a torn-tail. They would swim past them, swishing their tails in their faces and circle round and round them at high speed. "You're a stupid torn-tail, torn-tail, torn-tail, you're a stupid torn-tail," they would screech. "Well, aren't you?" they'd say. "Admit it, stupid, what are you? Tell me what you are, go on, say it… Say it."

Then they would swim faster and faster around the poor torn-tail until it would put its head down, feeling deeply ashamed of its pitiful existence and whisper: "I'm a stupid torn-tail."

Then the other fish would laugh out loud: "Ha, ha, reeeeeeee-zult!" they would shout happily and dart off through the water, swishing their tails a considerable amount more than was necessary.

The torn-tails were always very sad but being treated in this way made things even harder for them. They actually weren't stupid, in fact most of them were very intelligent. The difference was that they did not pretend to know about things that they actually had no idea about. Unfortunately though, having been made into torn-tails, they began to believe that they were stupid and deserved to be punished.

Oceans Apart

So the bottom of the sea really wasn't a great place to live. The fish spent their time swimming around fin to fin to avoid attacks by enemy fish. "The enemy is always waiting for you," the King and Queen would frequently say to them, "and the moment you forget that, it will have you. We must stick together unless we wish to be someone else's food." So the fish moved around in a fearful shoal with the torn-tails following behind so they would only get to eat what the others didn't find. Slowly they would drift, scouring the area through heavy, darkened eyes.

And so it was that all the fish stuck together, terrified of being split from the shoal by the enemy. Life was not only made rather unpleasant by this mentality, it was also incredibly boring.

This apparently normal way of life had yet to be questioned by a fish, until that was, a distinctly unusual fish began her life. Her name was Jura and she was a good size and shape with wide, inquisitive eyes. An unspoken feeling rippled through the waters that day, signalling mild disturbance. As soon as she joined the shoal she was immediately troubled by constant distraction. Jura wanted to look at everything that she passed and often stopped to absorb it. To her, this was natural curiosity not misbehaviour but she was soon to discover that she was alone in this way of thinking. The other fish informed her harshly that her inquisitive nature was not going to be tolerated. She would find her state of wonder brutally interrupted by a harsh nudge in the tail, propelling her at great speed into the centre of the shoal. Jura found it not only intensely irritating but also quite painful. Her new fragile form became battered and bruised as she hurtled into a mass of angry fish.

Jura was only a few days old when she did the unforgivable. She swam eagerly up to the King and Queen with an innocence the other fish could barely comprehend. "Tell me," she said, "why is it we always swim in the same place? Let's see what's up there," and she swung her body vertically. "I bet there's lots more food there." And with that, she launched herself upwards, excited by this good idea she had. The other fish stayed still, utterly shocked by the cheek of the newcomer.

"Tell me my ears are deceiving me," the King snarled at the Queen. The other fish cast their eyes downwards so as not to draw any attention to themselves. The King was angry and if they were not careful they would all have to suffer. Jura looked down questioningly at the King. She was genuinely confused and did not know what was upsetting him like this. His eyes flashed angrily at her. "How dare you!" he bellowed, "come back down at once." Jura obediently swam down to the King. "You are three days old," he said, "and after three whole days you feel that you know more about the ocean than I do. ME – THE KING." His voice sent angry vibrations through the water, causing a slight stinging sensation to settle on Jura's scales.

"No that wasn't what I meant, I was just saying that maybe we should be looking…"

The King cut her short. "I know full well what you were saying, you were trying to undermine my authority. Trying to tell me that I don't know what's best for my shoal." His eyes darted to and fro angrily.

"It was just a suggestion," Jura replied in a desperate attempt to defend herself. The other fish knew it was an error; they were now more frightened for Jura than she was for herself as they had seen what the King was capable of. He stared into Jura's eyes with a mixture of deep disappointment, resentment and aggravation. The intensity of it sent a physical pain through her and she turned her head away. No sooner had she averted her eyes from his than he lunged his teeth into her tail. She screeched in pain and shot forward in shock, causing his teeth to tear through her tail.

"Congratulations," he sneered, "you're a torn-tail at three days old, I can see you'll go far." And with that, he let out an evil jeer.

"This one has a few things to learn," spat the Queen, staring at Jura with a look of disgust. "To the sel," she shouted in the direction of the main shoal. They all just continued staring as if hypnotised. "NOW!" hollered the Queen and 10 of the longer, beefier, meaner looking fish shot out from the shoal and surrounded Jura.

The fish encased her with a brutal strength that she knew she had no chance of resisting. Their bulky, hardened bodies clamped themselves around her tightly. They moved through the water like one big entity, barely distinguishable as individual fish at all. Jura hurt all over from being crushed and also from a feeling of confusion that she knew she could not voice. Through the water they ploughed and she began to long to arrive at her destination, wherever it was, if only to stretch her body out and feel water around her again. She would never have wished to be there though if she had had any idea where she was heading.

CHAPTER 2
A long way down

After what seemed like an eternity, they arrived. The two large fish in front of Jura moved to one side, bringing into view a large, dark mound. In front of the entrance was an obese black and grey-striped eel with small, sharp red eyes like a lump of blubber with attitude. "Aha," he said, "what have we here? Fresh blood, I see, good, good." With that, he winked at the fish surrounding Jura and in an instant they disappeared. As soon as they had gone, Jura was left with only this red-eyed creature for company and rather wished the others would come back. She felt the sudden release of their pressure combined with the unnerving glare of the red eyes a little disconcerting to say the least. The thought of swimming away from this creature, however, was not an option; the look in his eyes erased any possibility of that. The eel was so ugly, Jura could hardly bear to look at him. He was one of those creatures that didn't need to say anything, his eyes said more than enough. In fact, they said so much that it felt impossible to move. He evidently did not feel the need to move his fat body even at the sight of 'new blood'. He just looked at her hungrily and with a glint in his eye that she tried hard not to focus on.

Jura stayed still, her newly torn tail throbbing. She could feel the water in the tear; it was a curious sensation. When she moved her tail from side to side, the water just slipped through it. Her attention was temporarily distracted by this unfamiliar feeling. She began to wonder if she could actually swim but did not feel this was the time or the place to experiment. No wonder this monstrous creature didn't seem to be remotely concerned that she might swim away.

The fat eel slowly opened his mouth and gurgled: "Tristor, a fresh one," and a fish grey in both body and demeanour appeared. Jura was grateful for the distraction from those piercing red eyes but the sight of Tristor was perhaps more painful still. Her eyes met what she would have thought was a fish corpse if he hadn't been swimming. He was so emaciated she could see his bones sticking through his skin. In fact, he looked like a fish carcass surrounded by a grey shadow. His sunken eyes peered out from their sockets and into Jura's with an expression so blank that she could have read whatever she wanted into it. Both his body and mind had been eaten away. Just looking at this poor creature made Jura feel sad.

Oceans Apart

Whatever could have happened to him?

Her thoughts were abruptly interrupted by the fat, red-eyed eel. "Get on with it then," he shouted at Tristor, "take her down." Tristor signalled to Jura with his eyes and she knew she must follow.

She swished her tail, forgetting that it was now torn but the realization hit her strongly as the water whooshed through it. Back and forth she swung her tail but it was no good. She started to panic and move it faster in the hope that she'd at least be able to get somewhere but it soon became clear that swimming was an impossibility. A sharp, searing sensation travelled through her body and although she knew her attempts to swim were pointless, admitting that it was hopeless somehow felt even harder. In her frantic state, she had not noticed that the eel was grinning excitedly at her struggle. A feeling of confusion and anxiety spread through her. She hadn't thought about swimming before, it was just something that happened. There was no need for her to learn how to, it had just felt like the most natural thing in the world for her to do. But now she was a torn-tail she was beginning to see that things would be very different now this instinctual ability had been severed.

"Nice try, runt," sniggered the fat eel. "Not so easy now, is it?" and he broke into a loud cackle that wobbled his blubber before echoing through the water. Tristor's eyes were downcast. He couldn't bear to see it happen to another fish but he knew it was inevitable. After Jura had writhed around for long enough for the fat eel to know she realized she couldn't escape, he nodded in Tristor's direction. "I think that ought to clarify matters," he said. "The rest she'll learn down there." Tristor brought his eyes back up to Jura's and gave her a look which told her he understood. This was partly comforting for Jura but also worrying. Tristor's corpse-like form was hardly a reassuring one and what he must have been through to be in this state didn't bear thinking about.

Tristor drifted over to Jura with a long reed in his mouth that he had picked up from the entrance to the mound. As he swam past her he saw her distraught expression and whispered, "don't worry, I'm not going to hurt you. This will help you for now, just stay still." Jura kept her eyes ahead of her, wondering what on earth was going on. Questions flooded her mind but she knew right now they were not going to be answered. For now, the only option was to do as she was told and hope for the best. She jumped suddenly as she felt the reed make contact with her broken tail. Slowly she felt it being wrapped round and round and then being tucked in under itself. "There you go," he said, moving back around in front of her, "now follow me and stay close behind." Jura complied and with a flick of her tail was surprised to feel that the water no longer passed through it at all. The reed did feel rather tight and restricting but at least it enabled her to move. The eel turned to Jura. "Collect three silver shells and you'll be accepted back," he said, "but without them you shall never return to the ocean."

Jura sighed and felt as if a lead balloon was inflating inside her. Slowly and reluctantly she followed Tristor into the black mound. There was an eerie presence inside. It was cold and dark. The water was murky and grey and it was difficult to see where she was going. "Just stay on my tail," Tristor whispered as they moved towards what looked like an entrance to a tunnel. Jura's heart was thumping against her bones, causing her vision to blur from the vibrations travelling through her body. It was truly horrible; the darkness seemed to have her on a leash and was slowly drawing her in.

The tunnel was barely wider than they were but Tristor seemed familiar with the route and was confident that they would fit through. It was dirty and smelt so bad Jura was reluctant to breathe but unfortunately she had no choice for this was no short tunnel. They wound their way down, twisting and turning their bodies as and when the tunnel demanded it. At times it became so thin that Jura scraped her scales on the cold walls. Tristor found it easier as he was so much thinner and he waited patiently for Jura as she navigated the narrow sections. "Where are we going?" she whispered. Even though there was no one around, she felt the need to speak softly.

"Sshh," responded Tristor. "Don't ask questions I cannot answer, just follow me."

"I don't understand," cried Jura but Tristor didn't respond.

They snaked further and further through, the smell making Jura want to wretch. The tunnel spiralled in places, making her feel even more disorientated and dizzy and sometimes it dropped to another level with no prior warning. A medley of thoughts criss-crossed through her mind and barely had she begun to single them out when the walls of the tunnel pulled themselves away from her and suddenly she was no longer enclosed. The tunnel had come to an end and having gathered quite a momentum she was propelled out of its clasp. The dark water rushed past her eyes, making it impossible to see anything at all and she let out a yelp as her body collided with a large object. This caused a dim light in a murky ball to ignite, illuminating the cause of her bruised head. She glanced up and then floated back a metre or so for a better look. It was a black sign with white swirly writing inscribed on it.

Welcome to the sel, fish,

You may feel unprepared

But worry not, we're a friendly lot,

There's no need to be scared.

Just keep on swimming through, my friend,

You no longer need a guide.

This is the place to heal and mend

those caught in the divide.

Oceans Apart

Baffled by this bizarre inscription, Jura turned to Tristor for an explanation but he had vanished. Her eyes scanned the area urgently but he was nowhere to be seen. She called his name but there was no reply and her voice seemed to be swallowed up by the water. Again and again she tried but her efforts were fruitless. Her eyes darted to and fro but nothing could really be seen in the thick, dirty water. She hadn't a clue which direction to take. It all looked the same. A panicked and fearful tear formed and began to sting the corner of her eye before escaping and being absorbed by the water. What was she meant to do? For a brief moment she wished she was back with the shoal. At least she couldn't get lost up there and the water seemed positively clean in comparison to this. After continuing to call for Tristor in vain for a few more minutes, her eyes were drawn back to the sign. *Just keep on swimming through, my friend, you no longer need a guide*. It wasn't as if she had many other options, so she moved herself precariously around the sign and began to swim, keeping an eye out for Tristor. As she swam, more dimly lit balls ignited, allowing her to see the way.

The lights were so weak she had to strain her eyes to see where she was going. She could not see any walls around her, instead it was a wide, murky expanse with an eerie absence of boundaries. It felt like this thick water stretched forever on either side of her and in a way, down here it did. The water was bitterly cold and carried with it a strange smell which was slightly different to that in the tunnel but equally as unappealing. It smelt of stale fish and gave her a deep feeling of unease. She continued to swim through it nonetheless, her insides wincing at the atmosphere she had been thrown into.

Her mind carried itself back to the ocean. How strange this all was. She was so confused as to why she had been sent here. Why had the King and Queen become so angry when she suggested that there might be more food for everyone higher up? It was a good idea and she knew it. And the silver shells, what could they be about? While she did not know what was ahead of her, she hoped that perhaps it would not be too bad here. The trouble was, she was a clever fish and as hard as she tried, if only to lift her dampened spirits, she could not convince herself that this place she had landed in was going to be fun.

As the fifth light ignited, Jura's attention was suddenly drawn to a cluster of bubbles that were emerging in the water directly ahead of her. She could see them clearly because they were black and although the water was dirty, they were certainly darker than it was. She stopped in her tracks to watch them. Hundreds more bubbles started to appear and popped at various points in front of her. Although the bubbles themselves were black, when they popped, the darkness dissolved in the water. It spread so quickly through the water that its source was soon unidentifiable. That was until the bubble bearer itself slowly came into view.

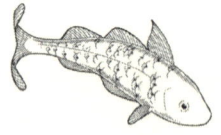

CHAPTER 3

Jura meets her menfish

Directly behind the flow of bubbles, a black fish emerged. For a split second, Jura thought it was Tristor. The fish was equally scrawny looking and obviously severely undernourished. There was no essence to her as there had been none to Tristor. They both owned the same shadowy, ghost-like presence. Her eyes had the same hollow look, a look that Jura was unsure whether to pity or distrust. As her eyes met the fish's, the hollowness instantaneously switched to a look of hunger. It reminded her of the way the fish in the shoal had looked when they had seen food. Her guard shot up as she sized up this somewhat intimidating, spectral figure.

Jura's alarm was evidently no better concealed than the other fish's look of hunger. The fish opened her mouth, producing a rush of black bubbles that Jura instinctively shied away from. "Oh little one, you mustn't be scared of me, relax, you're safe here. My name is Madame Aegrus and I have come to welcome you to the sel. You must be Jura."

"Er yes, yes I am," replied Jura a little hesitantly.

"Well I'm pleased to meet you," continued Madame Aegrus, "good journey here?"

Jura thought back to the stinking tunnel, the darkness and the fear of where she was going. "Um, not really no," she replied. "In fact, if I'm honest with you, it was quite horrible."

Madame Aegrus looked at her patronizingly. "Oh dear, dear, dear," she said, propelling more black bubbles in Jura's direction. "I can see what they meant, you really do have a lot to learn. Oh well, I suppose you're only young, aren't you? Every new fish is a challenge, little one, that's what I say."

Jura's confusion was escalating. 'A lot to learn', 'new challenge', whatever did she mean?

"Come, come," Madame Aegrus continued, "we'll have you settled in no time. Let's go and meet the others, shall we?"

"Hang on a minute," cried Jura. "Where am I and where are we going?"

"Didn't you see the sign?" replied Madame Aegrus, flicking her wispy tail and twisting round to face the direction she had come from. "You're in the sel, now follow me."

"I know that," Jura shouted after her, "but what is it?"

"Just follow," Madame Aegrus replied a little

impatiently. Jura stubbornly stayed still. She had just followed one withered fish down here with no explanation, she'd be damned if she was going to do it again.

"Not until you tell me where I'm going," she responded.

Madame Aegrus stopped and slowly turned around. "You're a right little worrier, aren't you, little one? Trust me, you've nothing to fear, now if you'll just stay behind me, I'll show you around." Jura paused for a moment and soon came to the conclusion that unless she wanted to investigate this murky under-sea place alone, she would have to follow Madame Aegrus. Although she was reluctant to follow a second fish who would not answer her questions, she decided that was the lesser of the two evils.

Jura swam close behind her, watching the black bubbles popping on either side of them and then mysteriously disappearing. They passed through murkier and murkier water until it became so thick with dirt it was difficult to swim through, especially with a makeshift tail. It quickly became very tiring and although Jura was putting all her energy into moving her tail, she felt she was barely getting anywhere. She struggled along nonetheless, desperately trying to keep up with Madame Aegrus, who didn't appear to be finding it a problem at all. In fact, she was positively gliding through it. "Wait for me," shouted Jura, gasping for oxygen, for there was so little of it. Madame Aegrus had evidently forgotten that new fish are not accustomed to swimming in such murky water.

"Oh I am sorry, little one," she called back. The thick water muffled Madame Aegrus' shout to a whisper.

"Well, you're obviously not," thought Jura, "if you were then you'd surely wait." For Madame Aegrus had continued swimming at exactly the same pace without slowing down one bit.

Jura was becoming more and more tired as she fought her way through the virtually impenetrable water. Her whole body ached from the strain of it. Swimming here drained everything out of you, partly because of the lack of oxygen but also due to the effort involved in driving your way through it. Madame Aegrus shouted back to Jura again. "Come on, we all find it difficult at first but you'll be used to it before you know it." She was too far ahead to see Jura's expression, which is probably just as well. It was the last thing Jura wanted to hear at that moment. She wanted to get out of this place, not used to it.

Jura's mind darted manically around. She knew life under the rule of the King and Queen was deeply wrong but this? This felt even worse. She kept trying to tell herself that perhaps it wouldn't be so bad once she got there but she couldn't help but believe it would be. She couldn't imagine the water suddenly changing drastically or even the atmosphere. And this Madame Aegrus, what was she all about? Her thoughts were interrupted when she came to an abrupt halt on Madame Aegrus' tail. In front of them both there stood a large, rusty, metal door. It was as if it had appeared out of nowhere. Madame Aegrus turned around to face a rather tired and withdrawn-looking Jura. "It's all right," she said, "we're here now". Jura did not reply. She did not want to waste the little oxygen she had. "Cheer up," continued Madame Aegrus. Jura forced a smile. There were many things she wanted to say but chose to keep them to herself. She did not want to aggravate the only fish she knew down here.

Madame Aegrus swung herself around and spoke quietly through the rusty keyhole. Jura could not understand a word of what she said. Within a matter of seconds, Jura heard a key turning in the lock and then the door crept open slowly as if the fish behind it was expecting an unwelcome visitor. Madame Aegrus slid through the gap, beckoning Jura to follow.

Her eyes met with those of a large, shiny, black lobster with claws so thick and sharp she knew he wasn't one for messing with. His eyes were small and beady and they pierced through the dirty water so brightly they were almost like lights. He directed them at Jura and stared at her for a moment. She looked blankly back at him, unsure what he was expecting. Although perhaps she should have felt intimidated by this, she was too tired to and was more concerned with what they were planning on doing with her.

Without warning, his mood changed entirely and a huge smile began to spread across his face. "Hello-ello-elloww," he gargled and scuttled around behind Jura. She felt his claw squeezing in between her tail and the reed that was holding it together. Then she simultaneously heard and felt a short, sharp snip. Her tail fell loose. Jura flinched nervously. She had got used to the feeling of the reed wrapped around it; it was holding her together, if only temporarily. After feeling so totally useless and incapable when her tail had been torn, the reed was a comfort. It enabled her to do the one thing that was vital as a fish: swim. "You won't be needing this down here," said the lobster, flicking the reed from his claws with a look of slight distaste. "In the sel, we see no need for such accessories."

Jura couldn't face moving her tail and feeling the water seep through it again. She did not need a reminder of how hopeless it made her feel so she kept it as still as she could. "Right now," said the lobster, sizing Jura up with his piercing eyes, "I see your bubbles are running clear, which is disappointing, but we've time to work on them and I suppose you are young so not to worry too much." The fish in the shoal were strange enough but this was like another language. It was as though she was expected to understand what he was talking about. "You're hardly our ideal size either – a little plump I might say, but that shouldn't be too difficult to rectify. Your main purpose down here, however, is far more important than your size or your bubble colour, although they will help us to monitor your progress. You are here to learn about your position in the ocean. It would appear that there has been a little confusion about this matter and this is the place where certain things are straightened out. When this happens you will have your silver shells as proof and will be set free. That is all you need to know at the moment, the rest will become clear with time. Now, I understand you are tired, you've had a long journey but just let me introduce you to your menfish and to me of course. I am sorry, how very rude of me. I don't believe I told you, Lord Skumble's the name," he announced and twiddled his claws proudly. "Yes, it really is me. I guess you've probably heard the name before, I'm pretty well-known but no need to feel embarrassed that you didn't already know. I'm in a good mood today so I'll forgive it." Jura had never heard his stupid name before and didn't much care about it or him either. "Madame Aegrus, will you go and fetch Engano for me immediately?" continued Lord Skumble.

Madame Aegrus disappeared in an instant into the murky water. "Who is she getting?" asked Jura. "Your menfish," Lord Skumble replied. Jura looked questioningly at him but said nothing. "Like a mentor, I suppose," he continued. "He will be the one that you'll need whenever you want to swim anywhere. To put it simply, he will be your tail. Without him it will be impossible for you to swim at all." The idea of this made Jura feel nervous. She wasn't sure about having to depend on another fish quite so heavily and hoped he'd be friendly. Jura was too tired to worry much more; she could hardly keep her eyes open. Although she resisted it, before long she'd drifted off into a deep sleep.

Jura wasn't sure how long she'd been asleep when she was suddenly jolted into consciousness by Engano tugging at her tail. "Wake up, sleepy tail, wake up, wake up," he shouted, his voice seeping into her unconscious like a shrill alarm clock. She was so tired though, and tried with all her strength to block it out but after a few frustrated minutes of resisting his plea she peeled open a weary eye. "At last," he shouted,

"Sleeping Beauty has arisen." Her eyes met first with a cloud of dark greenish-grey bubbles and then, as they gradually began to pop, he came into view.

There in front of her was an average-sized green fish with a little grey dappled here and there. He looked a little thin and perhaps slightly scrawny but not nearly as much as Tristor and Madame Aegrus did. His pale eyes looked eager, his face excitable. He looked at Jura and beamed a charming smile in her direction. She felt a little nervous but strangely optimistic. She thought he could have looked a lot worse. He introduced himself and did a few energetic twirls in the water to impress her. "Sorry to have woken you but I just couldn't wait to meet you," he said. "I'll leave you for now and come and collect you in the morning. Now you have a good night's sleep." Jura was so weary, this brief introduction still felt like part of her dream but she smiled and sunk back into the deep sleep that was pulling at her as strongly as the current that brought her down here. She slept all night long, disturbed by nothing. She did not stir when Madame Aegrus and Lord Skumble were talking. She did not stir when Lord Skumble was rearranging his reed collection. She did not even stir when the shrimps came in to clean. She was dead to the world.

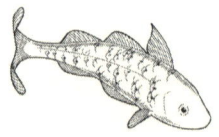

CHAPTER 4

A bit of common courtesy

When Jura awoke the next morning, Engano was already by her side. "Wow," he said as soon as he saw her eyes open, "the journey here really took it out of you, didn't it?" As he spoke, hundreds of greeny-grey bubbles scattered in Jura's direction.

"I guess it did," she replied, scanning the area around her with her newly refreshed eyes. Lord Skumble was counting something in the corner that Jura could not make out. He seemed to be deeply focused on whatever it was and appeared to have already lost interest in Jura's presence. She had been passed on to her menfish now.

Engano tucked Jura under his fin and swam off with her. "Oh, I'm so happy to have a new fish under my fin," he said to her. "I've been waiting so long for this privilege. I've been down here for ages you know, waiting and hoping to be honoured like this. He thinks I'm up to the job now. Lord Skumble has trusted me at last and I'm going to show him how capable I am. Oh Jura, you're too young to understand, but to be given the responsibility of showing a torn-tail the right direction is an honour I could only have dreamt of. I must show him how well I can do. You will help me, won't you?"

Jura couldn't quite understand what Engano meant by helping him but could see how much this meant to him and the excitement and enthusiasm shining in his eyes made her want to do whatever she could. Well, that and the fact that he was now her tail. "I'll do what I can," she replied.

Being carried along through the murky water was a huge relief after the struggle of swimming through it the previous day. The thought of carrying herself and another fish through it made her feel weak. She suddenly felt a flicker of admiration run through her scales as she contemplated how strong Engano must be. It was also much easier to breathe when you weren't actually swimming at the same time so she nestled under Engano's fin and peered out at the surroundings. It really was a strange place she had found herself in. The little lights continued to ignite, dimly showing them the way. Before long, Jura's eyes were drawn to something green in the distance. She immediately recognized the colour as it was exactly the same as Engano's bubbles. As they drew closer, the green mass that had at first been no more than a blur through the dirt, began to take shape. It was an enormous, green bubble. This bubble was slightly transparent and Jura could see some dark shapes floating inside. Engano drew to a halt. "This is where I leave you," he said, "there are things here for you to learn. I'll be right here when you come out so don't you worry, it's just not for me to enter the bubble anymore. Now in you go and I'll see you shortly." With that, he gave Jura a strong push and she burst through the skin of the bubble, causing it to wobble. She came face to face with about 20 other little torn-tails and a fierce-looking fish facing them all. Similarly to Tristor and Madame Aegrus, this fish looked unnervingly corpse-like.

All the eyes turned to her at once and she longed to be swallowed up by the dirty water. "That was rather an abrupt entrance for such a little fish," exclaimed the fierce-looking fish, whose bubbles were the exact same colour as the bubble they were in. "What do you say for interrupting us so unceremoniously?"

Jura felt herself tensing up. She couldn't think straight with all those eyes on her. "Er, it wasn't my fault," was what came out. "My menfish pushed me."

"So you're blaming your menfish for your rude interruption?" the fierce fish responded.

"Well, he pushed me, I couldn't have burst through like that on my own, look," Jura said and swung herself around exposing her torn tail, pleased that she had evidence to back up what she had said.

"That is hardly the point," snapped the fish, "now apologize at once for your rudeness."

"Sorry," Jura heard coming from her mouth, although she wasn't sure how it got there because she certainly wasn't.

"And as your punishment for your disruptive entrance you must stay where you are, separate from the rest of the group so the others can all be reminded of how not to behave and hopefully learn a lesson from it." Jura wished all the other fish would stop looking at her, it really wasn't helping the situation.

"Right now, where were we?" the stern fish continued as Jura looked around, taking in her new environment. "Oh actually, I suppose I should introduce myself to the latecomer. My name is Oprimir. Would you like to tell the group your name?" This wasn't a question although it sounded like one.

"It's Jura," she said nervously, her voice a little shaky.

"Right, well, now that's done we can get on with it, can't we? As I was saying, you are all here because you have disgraced the shoal in some way. Nine out of ten times it's due to lack of respect or just plain ignorance, both of which are traits I despise in a fish. It is a dangerous place up there in the ocean and the sooner you realize that, the better. Your King and Queen are experienced in the dangers and are there to protect you. They have devoted their whole lives to the upbringing of the shoal and expect to be treated with the respect they deserve. I don't really think that's too much to ask for, is it? They have hundreds of fish to look after. Try to imagine for a minute how kind and utterly devoted they must be to take on that commitment. Can any one of you see yourself giving up your own life to help hundreds of other lives?"

Oprimir paused and glared at all the torn-tails patronizingly. "I didn't think so," she snarled.

"The sel was founded thousands of years ago by an ancestor of Lord Skumble. A wise lobster, he was. He realized that any disruption to the shoal by means of disrespect or otherwise was a danger to the livelihood of the whole ocean. So he came up with the idea of the sel as a place where the misbehaving fish would come and be taught a few necessary lessons. How are you finding it down here so far?" Oprimir directed the question at a tiny little fish that looked eager to learn.

"Um, dark and horrible," the little fish replied.

"Well you won't survive long in the ocean with that attitude," said Oprimir, "anyone else?"

"Cold and murky," replied another.

"Not very friendly," another called out.

"No wonder you were all sent down here," Oprimir bellowed. "You really haven't got a clue have you? Have you ever heard of the phrase 'common courtesy'?" All the fish looked blank. "I guessed not," continued Oprimir. "It's lucky I'm thick-scaled or I might have got a little offended by those comments, did any of you stop to think about that? This is my home, is it not? I may become a little angry if other fish insult the place that I live. 'Cold and murky', what were you thinking?" Oprimir darted over to the little fish that had answered this and pushed her out in front of all the others.

"Right," said Oprimir, "I think it is perfectly clear to see why this fish is a threat to the shoal, isn't it?" No one answered. "It seems obvious to me and hopefully it will be to you before too long, that while you are in a fish's home water you do not insult them. Cold and murky are hardly complimentary, are they?" The little fish froze. "Well, are they?" shouted Oprimir, bombarding the fish with an explosion of green bubbles.

"Nnn-nno," stuttered the little fish.

"But it's true," added Jura, unable to contain her irritation. "It is cold and murky, everyone can see that. The water is so thick and dirty you can barely breathe."

"I knew you were trouble," snarled Oprimir, flicking her tail so she spun round to face Jura. "Try as hard as you dare to make me look stupid but believe me, you will always come off worse than I. I'm pretty respected down here so you had better learn to remember that. I'm not going to tell you what would have been a more appropriate answer, that is up to you to discover." She turned to the rest of the fish, "but what I will say to all of you is to think about what you are saying and who you may upset, anger or distress in any way. You'd better think quickly because not one of you will be eating today until you can think of an appropriate answer to my question." A cold shudder of fear rippled through the water.

"Clear and fresh," came a voice from the group.

Oprimir swam over to the fish who had complied. A smile spread across her gaunt face. "You're not as stupid as you look, Taimado," she said. "I like the sound of that, it makes me feel good." The fish who had responded was small and flat with eyes that darted to and fro. Eyes that were watching every movement around him like a hawk. Jura didn't like what he was up to, in fact it made her feel a bit sick. Oprimir was telling them to lie and she knew she was no liar. "You won't be down here for long," Oprimir said to Taimado. "I can see you're a quick learner. In fact, as an example to the group, I think you can go now. Go back to your menfish and tell him Oprimir says you can have second helpings of algae today." She then pulled him from the group and pushed him out through the bubble.

Oprimir turned back to the others. "It can be as easy as that for all of you, you know," she said. "Just a little consideration is all that's needed at this point." Jura could not believe how each fish in the bubble turned against that which they knew to be right in order to appease Oprimir. She was so disturbed by it that by the time she had listened to 20 sickly sweet lies she had lost her appetite anyway. There was no way that she was going to pretend this place was anything other than disgusting and she was horrified that the others were so willing to.

When at last she was the only fish left in the bubble Oprimir turned to her. "Well then," she shouted, "are you really so stupid that after hearing 20 times what you must do, you still have no idea how to get out?" And she laughed meanly in Jura's face. The bubble seemed to echo a little now all the other fish had gone.

"I know full well what you want me to say," said Jura bravely, "but I won't".

"What do you mean, you won't?" snarled Oprimir, "you've got a voice, haven't you?"

"Yes," replied Jura, "of course I have a voice but I am not going to use it to tell you what you want to hear when it's a lie".

"LIE," bellowed Oprimir. "Who ever mentioned anything about lying? I'm merely teaching you to learn a bit of respect." She started to shake from shock and anger. "I can hardly believe it, I'm being accused of lying by a torn-tail. I can certainly see why you had your tail torn, I've never met such an ignorant fish in all my born days. I feel deeply sorry for your menfish, no menfish should be subjected to this." Her speech sped up as she became more and more angry. "I tell you, you've got a lot to learn before you'll be released from here and if you want it to be in your lifetime I'd start thinking about your attitude."

"My attitude," thought Jura, but was careful not to say it. She could not believe what Oprimir was saying to her. She had not done anything except say she would not lie and anyone would have thought she had committed the biggest crime in the ocean.

"Get out of my sight," shouted Oprimir, "and for your own sake as well as everyone else's, come back with the desire to learn, at least." With that she pushed Jura forcefully back through the bubble.

Out she shot, her head full and confused. She was desperate to tell Engano about what had happened. He would understand. He was there as he had said, waiting patiently for her. "How was your first lesson?" he asked excitedly.

"Horrible," Jura replied and tucked herself under his fin.

"Oh come on," he said, "it can't have been that bad. Listen, let's take you to your thinking quarters."

They swam off slowly through the darkness. Jura's mind was still in the green bubble with Oprimir. There was so much she wanted to say to her but knew she couldn't and that made her want to say it even more. She wanted to tell Engano as well but sensed his mind was on other things and she did not want to annoy him too. They swam on and on, ploughing through the heavy water, passing nothing that Jura could make out. It was too dirty to see anything. Jura's mind felt as full of thought as the water was dirty. After an indistinguishable length of time, rows and rows of little cages slowly started to seep into her vision. Engano stopped. "This is the thinking quarters," he told her. "Each little fish is given their own thinking box, the whole thing especially for them. It's their own house, if you like. This is where you'll spend your time when you're in the sel. Well, the time that you're not in lessons, that is. Lord Skumble feels that the thinking boxes are essential in that they not only house the occupants down here but they also provide a space where valuable thinking can be done."

Jura glanced down at the rows upon rows of cages, the majority of which were occupied, with their menfish waiting outside. She felt a pulse of anxiety beat through her and Engano felt it. "Don't worry, Jura," he said. "I know it doesn't look like the most comfortable of places but Lord Skumble was never one for extravagances. They're not so bad though. Come on, let's go and find a nice one for you, shall we?" They moved slowly past menfish, cage and occupant, menfish, cage and occupant. The more caged fish Jura saw, the less comfortable she felt. She noticed that all the menfish blew out exactly the same colour green bubbles.

"I don't want to be in a cage," she told Engano as the tension increased inside her body.

"It's not a cage," he said, "it's a thinking box. You can come out for a swim with me whenever you want but much of your time down here must be spent thinking and after all, you need a place to do that thinking. Honestly, Jura believe me, new environments are always a bit daunting but I'll be here with you."

After they had passed about 30 of these thinking boxes, almost all of which were occupied, they reached two empty ones next to each other. Jura liked the idea of having an empty box beside her, it made hers seem more spacious. Engano stopped and turned to her. "Here we go, this one looks like a good one to me," he said and nudged her in gently. "I'll be right here if you need me. You gather your thoughts and I'll tell you when it's time for your next lesson."

This had all been so much for Jura to take in. She needed some time to think. Her thoughts, however, did not revolve around her behaviour, as she supposed they were meant to, for she knew she had done nothing to be ashamed of. Instead, she went over the events of the past few days. She was beginning to realise that there were a lot of very strange fish out there that were living in a way that she just knew wasn't right. The whole atmosphere in the sel, the lack of oxygen and the denseness of the water was enough for Jura to realize that this was not a place that encouraged life. She thought back to Tristor and quivered as she remembered his haggard form. She wondered what had happened to him. Maybe he had been released, his duties completed. Did that mean that she would have to be that emaciated before they would allow her to return to the ocean? And Madame Aegrus, she seemed to have some authority and she too looked like that… And Oprimir. Jura felt herself beginning to panic. She wanted to get out of there but not if it meant becoming like them. Her mind began to spiral downwards like the tunnel that had brought her here. "Oprimir hates me already," she thought. "I've barely been here two minutes and I've already annoyed her. What's going to happen to me?" Her head started to hurt as she worried about what lay ahead of her. She stewed over worse-case scenarios for the whole of her thinking period and was eventually jolted out of this state by Engano tapping at her cage.

"Come on, we'll be late," he said, and opened the cage.

CHAPTER 5
Shell, shock

Engano tucked Jura under his fin and off they set back through the oppressive waters. Each direction looked the same. There was no knowing where you were heading down here. She only knew they were going somewhere else because they turned left out of the cage instead of right. They swam for about 10 minutes before reaching another large bubble. This one was dark red. When they arrived there were about 12 other torn-tails saying goodbye to their menfish before entering the bubble. Jura recognised some of them from her previous lesson but was in no mood for socialising. In fact, she wasn't really interested in getting to know the other fish down here, she was more concerned about getting out.

Oceans Apart

"See you later then," said Engano and pushed her off into the red bubble. Jura was inside it before she had a chance to reply.

At least she wasn't late this time. There were a few other torn-tails in there and more following behind her. Directly ahead of her stood a red crab with cloudy grey eyes and sharp, thin, pointy claws. He glared at each fish as they entered the bubble with a look of intense disgust and fidgeted impatiently, scraping his claws together in a way that looked as if he was sharpening them. This crab made Oprimir look friendly.

Once all the torn-tails were inside the bubble, the crab spoke. As he opened his mouth, a mass of red bubbles emerged. "My name is Ira," he said, standing high on his pincers so he could look down on them all with an even greater sense of importance. "From what I've heard about you lot," he continued, "you're a bunch of rejects from the ocean." No one spoke. "You hardly need to look further than your torn tails to see that. You are the lowest of the low and must learn the rules that will help you to better yourself."

A few of the fish wriggled uneasily, Jura included. "Why must there be so many rules everywhere you look?" she thought. She really just wasn't interested in hearing them all.

Ira began to dig up the dirt ferociously. The fish watched in anticipation as the sand and silt flew out behind him. One or two of the fish looked across at each other questioningly. Ira dug like a dog searching hungrily for a bone it had buried earlier. Gradually, the fish started to see something small and red appearing.

As he continued to dig, it slowly became evident that there were more than one of these red objects, in fact, there seemed to be quite a few. Before long, a small pile began to emerge and he started to scoop them out with his claws. It soon became clear that these red objects were shells.

Ira lined them up at the opposite end of the bubble to the fish. There was one shell for every fish. When he had finished laying them out he quickly filled the hole back in. "Right," he said with a somewhat gleeful tone, "your task in here is to get yourself to one of those shells." Jura couldn't help but think what a ridiculous suggestion that was considering that he knew full well that their tails had been torn and they could not swim without their menfish. All the fish looked at each other and appeared to be equally baffled by this bizarre request. None of them moved because they couldn't. They stayed staring at the shells suspiciously whilst Ira looked at them expectantly. "Well, come on then," he said, after some time, "make some effort at least."

One by one the fish began to move their tails back and forth in the hope that maybe it would work but it was impossible, as Jura knew full well. They moved their tails faster and faster as Ira's glare intensified, all except Jura who knew what they were trying to do was futile. It did not take a genius to work that out. "Move!" shouted Ira, deeply angered by their incapacity to get anywhere at all. Tails swished faster and faster as the little fish put all their energy into this exercise. Jura decided it was probably a good idea not to draw attention to herself so slowly began to move her tail from side to side, just enough for it to be noticed that at least she was trying. The last thing she wanted was to be singled out again.

The more the fish struggled, the angrier Ira became until he started hurling insults at them individually. "Oi you, No-Brain, show us what you're made of." "Hey, Stubby Tail, got a problem moving, have you?" "You over there, you're so ugly I can't make out which end is your head and which is your tail." On and on he went, throwing out nastier and nastier insults. His anger seemed to be feeding off the torn-tail's fear. As Jura listened to these mean comments she felt herself beginning to twitch with fury. She could not believe the nerve of this crab. How could such an ugly, horrible creature put them all down in this way and get away with it? Who did he think he was? As all the other fish bowed their heads in shame, Jura held hers high. She would not allow him to make her feel stupid and ugly, even if the rest would.

When Ira reached Jura he began to insult her scales. "What's your problem, Scabby Scales?" he snarled. "We all know about you," he continued, "you're the one who thinks she knows better than the King and Queen. You're the one who thinks she's so important we should all listen to her, right? Well, you're small and insignificant and don't ever create any illusions in that small head of yours that suggest otherwise."

Jura could feel herself filling up with anger. With every word Ira said she felt her blood bubbling inside. The insults continued to fly at her like poisoned arrows and the more she heard, the more she could feel her anger writhing around inside her like a wild snake in a cage. Both the arrows and the snake were increasing in their intensity. She began to lose control. She could no longer hear what he was saying, she could only feel the strength of it. Suddenly, everything she could see turned red, bright red. The snake had escaped. She burst forward with an expulsion of energy that propelled her right over to the other side. She was taken directly to one of the shells and the instant she touched it, it turned silver.

It had happened so quickly she felt completely confused as to how she had got there. It certainly wasn't through trying to use her torn tail like the others had been doing, she knew that much. It was like a build-up of some immense force that had driven her through the water. Slowly, she turned around to face Ira and the rest of the group, unsure what kind of reaction she was going to receive. The other torn-tails gaped at her, looking a little unnerved. Ira, however, looked excited and no longer angry in the least. "Congratulations," he shouted in a tone entirely opposite to the one he had been using before. "A spectacular result, Jura, I must say you've proved yourself beyond belief. I for one am shocked to see that you had it in you and so quickly, on the first lesson in this bubble." Jura was stunned at the way Ira's anger at them all seemed to have dissolved as soon as she had reached the shell.

"Take the shell to your menfish," said Ira proudly, holding his claws wide apart in the air. "He will feel honoured to have such a fish under his fin." Jura looked suspiciously at the crab – she was wary of him.

How could he have changed entirely from one second to the next? It was not natural. She felt uneasy in the presence of such an unpredictable creature and was keen to get back to Engano. Fortunately, her wishes were granted and Ira scuttled over to her. "Come on," he said, "you've learned more than enough for one day". And with that he pushed her along to the edge of the bubble and nudged her gently through.

What exactly Jura was supposed to have learned she was not sure but she did know that something strange and slightly creepy had gone on in there. Something that deep inside her she knew was not right, despite Ira's outright approval of it. She felt something that she did not understand. She knew she had to collect shells in order to be released so surely she should be pleased that she had one? Somehow though, she felt she would rather not have the shell than please that horrible crab. Ira's mad mood twist happened because of what she had done and she distinctly disliked that thought.

Engano was waiting for her on the other side of the bubble. His face dropped when he saw her. "Oh no, what have you done?" he asked, his concern about her early exit from the bubble altering his voice. Jura opened her fin and slowly revealed the silver shell. Engano's eyes lit up and he spun around excitedly. "A shell, a shell," he sang. "Well, well, well, here in the sel, my little fish has got a shell." He swam around her tired body singing with such joy anyone would have thought it was him who had been given the shell and not Jura. After indulging his own excitement for a few minutes he stopped swimming around and faced her.

Oceans Apart

"I can't wait to tell Lord Skumble, he'll be so proud of you," he said. "Do you realise how clever you are?" Jura did not answer. She did not feel in the least bit clever, in fact the very opposite. She felt like she had entered something that she did not want to be part of and that, in her mind, was not clever. She tried not to show Engano how she was feeling. He seemed so excited and she did not want to spoil that. "I'm so proud of you," he continued, "so proud you wouldn't believe."

Jura must have hidden her feelings well for Engano did not appear to notice that she was not as excited as would be expected of a fish in her situation. Engano pulled her under his fin and headed off as fast as he could swim. Jura could feel the excitement in his every cell but as they ploughed through the dense water she became more and more drained. As they continued her body physically relaxed. In her fatigue she almost slid from his grasp. As his attention was drawn to her lack of energy he suggested that perhaps he should drop her off at the thinking boxes first and then take the shell to show Lord Skumble afterwards. Jura was relieved at the suggestion. She did not feel like showing off her shell to Lord Skumble anyway.

When they reached the thinking boxes most of them were empty as the other fish were learning their lessons. Outside the boxes, however, were hundreds of little pink shrimps moving through the water. It looked to Jura as if they were concentrating on something. "What are they doing?" she asked Engano, suddenly feeling a little more alert.

"I'm surprised you haven't seen them yet, they do all the cleaning down here."

Jura felt quite charmed by them, their little pink curly bodies wiggling along one after the other. She thought they looked rather endearing. "Hello," she called out at one as he passed. The little shrimp completely ignored her. He carried on, his eyes focused directly ahead.

Engano chuckled, "they're dead heads, silly," he said. "Deaf as posts, the lot of them and dumb too, can't hear or speak so they're not much good for anything but cleaning." Jura looked around her. The place was so dirty, cleaning down here really was no easy task. She looked behind her at the shrimps. They did not look overly inspired by their work but they certainly were not making a fuss about it. They just seemed to be doing the best they could in an almost robotic fashion.

When Engano had reached Jura's box, he placed her gently inside and then left with the shell to show Lord Skumble. Jura stared out at the shrimps as they passed rhythmically one by one like tiny, swimming soldiers. She found herself being drawn into a kind of hypnosis by them and as she watched them fading into the distance she was lulled into a gentle sleep.

When she awoke a little later on, all the shrimps had gone. She could not see any other fish near her although she could feel that they were there. Engano was back, waiting patiently outside her box. The moment he saw her wake his eyes lit up. "Oh Jura," he said, "Lord Skumble was so pleased as I knew he would be. So pleased for both you and me. I don't think he really believed that a torn-tail of mine could collect a shell so quickly. He said that if you carry on doing this well you'll be released back to the ocean before you know it. I brought some food with me for you. Here you go, have a munch on that." He passed through some delicious-looking algae that she ate gratefully. When she had finished, he opened up the box, swam in and began digging a hole with his tail. When he'd built a sizeable one he placed the shell inside. "Your shell is to stay in here for safe-keeping," he told her. "Once you've collected all three shells we shall take them out and present them to Lord Skumble. At that moment you shall be set free." Jura felt a shimmer of excitement tingle through her bones. "But until then, they must stay buried," he said, "that is the tradition of the sel."

Jura's third lesson took place in a large black bubble. She arrived in the same way as before but as she entered the bubble she was surprised to see a familiar face teaching the lesson. "We meet again," said Madame Aegrus. Jura was shocked to see her but as she thought about it, it made sense because Madame Aegrus' bubbles were certainly black and she was in a black bubble after all. She remembered them clearly, they were the first bubbles she had ever seen.

"Some of you I've seen before and some faces are new to me," Madame Aegrus began by saying. "Now let us begin. Focusing on your faults makes you a better fish. A humble fish will go far, an arrogant one – well that's another matter. As you've probably heard before, as it is a point that is stressed in the sel, we aim to give fish a realistic idea of their position in the ocean. Now the exercise for today is as follows: I would like you to each pick one thing about yourself that you dislike." She gave them a few seconds to think. "Right," she said, "now one by one I will bring you to the front and I want you to tell everyone what this is. To allow the fish in question to benefit from this exercise, the rest of you must laugh and make fun of the fish until they experience a feeling of shame. When this happens we find it creates a good grounding for the eradication of arrogance." Terror ran through the water and it stung their scales like vinegar. Jura was shocked at what a horrible task this was. She couldn't believe Madame Aegrus had told her she could trust her and that she had nothing to fear. She had failed to mention her own lessons.

"Not to worry, little ones," said Madame Aegrus, "it may not seem very nice but believe me it's for your own good and you'll thank me in the end. Arrogance is something we should eradicate before it grows." Jura was beginning to feel sick. She wanted to get out of the bubble, out of the sel completely. If she had known what was lurking down here she would never have suggested to the King and Queen that there may have been more food above. Although she still thought she was right, she now knew the price she was going to have to pay for speaking her mind. She could feel the pressure of the sel pushing her down like a lead weight.

"Right now, who's first?" Madame Aegrus' voice cut through her thoughts. All the fish, Jura included, avoided making eye contact with her. She waited a few painfully drawn-out seconds. "Oh dear, no one willing to learn? What a bunch I have here. Not to worry, I'll just have to choose..." She pulled out a terrified torn-tail from the class and placed her in front of all the others. It was the most horrible exercise Jura could have imagined. Each fish one by one exposed their weakest part to the class and had to try with all their heart to be brave while they were laughed and jeered at. Jura had hoped that because they were all in the same situation they wouldn't laugh too much but in fact the opposite seemed to happen. Their fear of Madame Aegrus was far stronger than their compassion for the rest of the class, or for themselves for that matter. The torn-tails were having their minds torn to match their tails.

When it came to Jura's turn she was so frightened that her mind felt like it had detached itself from her and was doing somersaults through the water. As Madame Aegrus pulled her to the front and she saw all the eyes focused on her, the bubble felt like it was closing in on her and she lost her ability to think at all. She hovered in the water, terror filling the space where her mind had once been. Her fear had taken over everything and she had forgotten why she was even there. The eyes watching her grew bigger and bigger until they filled up every inch of the bubble. One minute felt like a thousand lifetimes. She could not move, she could not think, she could not even see properly. The others were waiting for her to speak and the silence surrounding her grew a voice which was dark and thunderous. "Maybe it's your inability to speak," shouted Madame Aegrus through the dark silence. "That's hardly something to be proud of is it?"

Oceans Apart

The words swirled around her like frantic whirlpools distorting as they were sucked into the darkness.

"Or maybe it's her scales," suggested a torn-tail who had had her turn so had nothing more to lose.

"Perhaps her scraggly fins," came another and they all encouraged each other in the hope of gaining Madame Aegrus' approval.

The insults were being thrown at her like spears but it wasn't the words that hurt her, it was her own inability to speak that cut through her like a knife. Her mind now appeared to have dissolved like the coloured bubbles. She needed to swim away to a place where it would feel comfortable to reappear but with a torn tail there was certainly no chance of that.

Suddenly something inside her allowed her mouth to speak. "I hate my torn tail," came out quite unexpectedly. The jeering continued until Madame Aegrus felt Jura was in no danger of her arrogance spreading and returned her to the shoal. There she stayed until the class was over; eyes glazed, mind numb. The damage they were after had been done.

CHAPTER 6

Seven suggestions for serenity in the sea

Jura was so hurt by the experience in the black bubble that something inside her decided to switch off. When Engano came she collapsed limply behind his fin and when he asked if she was alright, she simply replied, "I'm fine". From that day on, things were never the same. The spark in Jura that had refused to be defeated by the injustice of it all fizzled out and she decided that it would be easier to give them what they wanted rather than have to go through that again.

For the next few nights she was haunted by flashbacks of Madame Aegrus' lesson. She could see all their mean faces distorting as they shouted at her and she felt her throat close up again and again. These images made it almost impossible for her to sleep. Her appetite also seemed to have abandoned her but she barely noticed. Hour after hour passed as she stared out blankly from her thinking box.

Her lessons continued regularly, alternating between the green and black bubble. She told herself that she must do whatever she could to collect these shells. Whenever she was tempted to voice an opinion she reminded herself of Madame Aegrus' lesson. The longer she stayed down here, the more she risked having to experience that humiliation again. By telling the teachers what they wanted to hear she was hurting herself just as much but at least if she was doing the damage she was in control of it. Well, that's what she told herself anyway. She began to spend time blanking her mind before each lesson in the hope that if she trained it not to think, it would be easier for her to remain obedient in the classes. When she was in the bubbles she would focus on agreeing and keeping any thought that escaped through the wall in her head strictly silenced.

Oprimir could not believe what she was seeing. Jura was a changed fish. As respect for her grew in the sel, this numbing of her mind was having a larger effect on Jura than she realized. She was losing weight rapidly and a cloudy veil had settled over her eyes.

The day before she earned her second shell, she almost let a slither of resistance expose itself but she caught it just in time. When she was telling Oprimir what beautiful eyes she had, she almost retched in objection to her insincerity, setting alarm bells off in her head. She must not tell the truth. The price she would have to pay was too high and she could not afford it. At the end of that lesson they had all been told to come up with what Oprimir had referred to as seven suggestions for serenity in the sea. Jura knew hers had to be good.

Jura spent all evening in her thinking box, wondering how she could combine everything she had been taught and prove to Oprimir that she was learning well. Although a few doubts popped into her head, when it was time for her next class she was fully prepared. She had been so deeply focused on remembering everything she had been taught, her real thoughts on the matter seemed to have been totally put to one side. She was on a mission to be set free from the sel.

That morning she urged Engano to swim faster to her lesson. The last thing she wanted was to be late. She needed Oprimir to be proud of her and nothing could go wrong. The lesson began and as each torn-tail reeled off their seven suggestions, Jura could sense Oprimir was getting more and more angry. After the fifth, she exploded: "Haven't you learnt anything down here? Now if you don't have any sensible suggestions then don't speak at all."

"I do, I do," Jura shouted and proceeded to reel off her seven suggestions for serenity in the sea.

1. Respect the King and Queen.
2. Obey their every command.
3. Believe and trust in them for they always know best.
4. Stay well within the boundaries set by them.

5. Remember your opinion counts for nothing.
6. Never venture away from the shoal. The enemy is always there.
7. Never suggest the possibility of a higher place existing in the ocean.

When she had finished she looked at Oprimir proudly, who looked back at her, astonished. Oprimir swam closer to her. "I struggle to believe that this is the same torn-tail that first entered my class in a manner of rudeness I shudder to recall. Can a fish who arrived in such ignorance really be saying such things? A fish that is so aware about what it is that will bring serenity to the sea must surely be worthy of a reward." She opened her fin and a shining silver shell twinkled and floated out towards Jura. This was surely confirmation that she was heading in the right direction, well the one that was going to get her released anyway.

"Two shells," Jura thought gleefully. "Just one more and I'm out of this horrible place forever." All her senses heightened for a split second at the mere thought of being set free. No more lessons, no more thinking boxes, no more Oprimir. Oh she couldn't wait. All she had to do was continue to tell them what they wanted to hear and she should have no problems.

For the rest of the lesson, Jura focused deeply on blanking any unacceptable thoughts. She didn't want to risk having her shell taken away again. She had no idea what the rest of the lesson was about, instead she floated off into a daydream about presenting Lord Skumble with her silver shells, about no longer having to live in water that was so thick with dirt you could barely see through it.

Although she was proud of herself for having been rewarded two shells, there was still a niggle inside her that prevented her from feeling truly happy but she knew she must ignore it to be free. The class ended and Oprimir started to push all the other torntails out of the bubble. She left Jura until last. When it was just the two of them she turned to Jura. "I'm glad you've chosen the right direction," she said. "We're all pleased for you." Jura felt a little nervous, she sensed there was more to come. "It hasn't escaped our attention, however, that your bubbles are still running clear. I'm not saying this is necessarily a problem seeing as you appear to be learning well despite this but it is rather unusual to say the least." Jura had been hoping it wasn't going to be brought up. "Now I am prepared to overlook this fact for I am beginning to see your potential in the ocean. Others, however, may see it differently. I just thought I should warn you that it hasn't gone unnoticed." This heightened the niggling inside Jura. She really did not need any unnecessary complications now things were going so well. As Oprimir pushed her out of the bubble she called after her: "Keep up the good work."

When she presented Engano with the second shell he could hardly contain himself but she didn't share his elation. She thought she would wait for Engano to stop doing somersaults in the water before mentioning the bubbles. Once she was under his fin she told him that there was something she needed to talk to him about. "Okay," he said, "let's wait until we've buried your treasure though, then my attention will be properly focused. At the moment my mind is rather distracted by this little gem, as you can probably see. I just want to make sure it's safe and then we'll have a chat."

Once Engano was satisfied that the shell was properly buried with the first he turned to Jura. "Right, what was it you wanted to talk about? I presume it's something to do with your achievement."

"Well, kind of," said Jura. She liked seeing her menfish in such high spirits and did not want to be the one to dampen them but all the same she felt she must tell him about her conversation with Oprimir. "It's my bubbles," she said. "They haven't changed colour once and I'm worried about what's being said. I mean, I know they're meant to change to the colour of the bubble I get the shell in but they're not, not at all. I mean not even once and Oprimir said that fish were noticing."

"Don't you worry about that," said Engano confidently. "Sure, it's a bonus if your bubbles change colour but you're collecting your shells, aren't you? It's the shells you need to be set free. Oprimir was probably just trying to scare you, she has a habit of doing that."

"But she said how pleased she was with me and how well I was doing. She wasn't being nasty to me at all," said Jura.

"She may not have seemed like she was but I'm afraid that's her style. Seeing how well you were doing probably unnerved her a little, that's all. Honestly, Jura, if I thought there would be any problems concerning your bubbles I would be the first to let you know. When we present Lord Skumble with your three shiny, silver shells the colour of your bubbles is not even going to enter his mind." Jura felt relieved. Engano seemed to put things back into perspective for her and after their conversation she allowed her bubble worries to fade.

A few days after their conversation, a new fish moved into the cage next to Jura's. Jura recognized her, she was one of the torn-tails who had been shouting at her so meanly in that horrible lesson with Madame Aegrus. The sight of her moving in instantly reminded Jura of that horrible experience. Up until then, she had not known any of the fish near her. They obviously had different lessons to learn and she was pleased about that. She didn't want anyone too close who knew things about her and especially not next door. The close proximity felt threatening.

The fish glanced in at Jura as it passed by and forced a smile from the corner of her mouth. "She might as well not have bothered," Jura thought to herself. A smile like that was more offensive than not smiling at all. For the first few days this fish did not say a word to Jura. Jura wished she would move thinking boxes, why had she moved here anyway? She instinctively disliked her. After she had been living there for about four days Jura decided that perhaps if she talked to the fish she wouldn't be so bad after all. She looked in at her one evening with a mixture of suspicion and curiosity. "Why did you move?" she asked.

The fish turned to Jura. "I was wondering when

you were going to talk to your new neighbour," she said. Jura felt a twinge of hatred towards the fish. She must at least try to give her a chance. The fish waited long enough to make Jura feel like shouting. She looked smug, enjoying keeping her waiting.

"Well?" said Jura, trying to sound calm.

The fish paused again, smiled to herself and finally replied, "Is that my business or yours?" Jura was quite shocked by this response and hesitated before replying: "Well, yours, I suppose," suddenly feeling a little embarrassed.

"Thank you," she said. "Now we've established that, I don't mind telling you. The truth is I thought I might be able to learn a thing or two from you, actually." Jura looked confused. "You're over halfway there, aren't you and I admire you for that. I haven't got any shells yet so you must be doing something right, eh?"

"I suppose I must be," replied Jura, feeling rather proud. She had not stopped to notice how many shells the other fish had. But no sooner had she begun to revel in her flattery than the other fish stole the compliment right back and took more with it.

"Mind you," the fish continued, "there is something I find somewhat mysterious about you, something that every fish is aware of down here and all have their own opinion about." She looked at Jura expecting a response but she gave none. "Your bubbles," she said, confirming Jura's worst fears. "Why don't they change?"

Jura knew this fish was up to no good and felt her hatred for her swell up inside her once more.

"How am I supposed to know?" she snapped defensively, feeling that having a constant reminder of the fact next door was the last thing she needed.

"You must know, they're your bubbles after all, not mine, not anyone else's." This fish was really beginning to annoy Jura.

"I don't know," Jura repeated, "and if you've just moved thinking boxes to find out then you might as well move back."

The fish stared at Jura with hard, disbelieving eyes. "Fine," she said, "don't tell me, but I'm warning you, I'm on your case. I can smell a fake a mile away so when I'm next door to it, it's more of a stench than a smell, if you catch my meaning. I'm telling you, you might as well just tell me now how you do it because I'll find out anyway."

Jura's mind and body suddenly felt a hundred times heavier. One more shell, she told herself, that's all she needed and then she'd be out, away from all this. Everything was so difficult down here. Just when she felt she was getting somewhere, this fish had to appear and make her doubt that. She told herself that she was doing the same as Oprimir – just trying to scare her. She must stay strong, stay focused on her final shell. She looked out to Engano. He was sleeping. Green bubbles scattered out in front of him with every exhalation. At least she had him; he would protect her from all these jealous fish. Jura decided to stop talking to the fish next door. The fish did not seem too bothered. She appeared to have said what she wanted to say and was now back in thinking mode but her presence still disturbed Jura.

Oceans Apart

As her lessons continued, Jura tried to focus on her obedience. She was becoming more practiced at blocking her mind before lessons and her opinions were making less and less of a fuss about being heard. She was determined to get her third shell. The days and nights seemed to be stretching themselves out and Jura's need to be released was greater than ever. She sometimes heard the other fish whispering about her in class, picking out the words 'Jura' and 'bubbles'. She reminded herself that they were just jealous of her and when she presented Lord Skumble with her shells she would be away from them all anyway. It was difficult though but she knew she must stay strong. Engano was a real comfort; he would always tell her not to worry what the other fish were saying and that if she wanted to collect her third shell she must not be distracted by jealous fish. She knew that but as hard as she tried, they were making her job a lot harder. Each night the fish next door looked at her in a way that made her nervous, making it impossible to relax.

CHAPTER 7

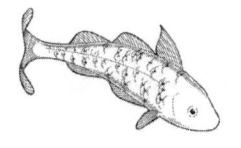

The rule of opposites

Jura still needed to collect a shell in Madame Aegrus' lesson and it worried her. However was she going to impress Madame Aegrus enough? Her pretence was going to have to be exceptional. It was one thing pretending in Oprimir's classes where she just had to say things she did not mean but in Madame Aegrus' class she had to be so brave. She would have to get over her fear of being laughed at and made to feel stupid because that seemed to be what Madame Aegrus wanted. Her classes had never been as bad since her terrifying experience but Jura still hated them passionately. She must learn to behave as if nothing was affecting her, to at least look like she was strong and could handle whatever was thrown at her. She decided to do whatever it was that Madame

Aegrus wanted. That's what she had done when she was given the other shells. She thought back to the first lesson with Ira. He had wanted her to take his anger and she did it. In the lesson with Oprimir she had wanted Jura to see the ocean as she did and she did it. Now she would have to work out exactly what Madame Aegrus wanted and give it to her. Simple as that.

She arrived at her next lesson with a new-born confidence. "No more resisting their ways," she told herself, before Engano pushed her into the black bubble, "I will be whatever she wants me to be." If she had known what Madame Aegrus had wanted, she may not have been quite so keen to obey.

"Right," said Madame Aegrus in a disconcertingly gleeful tone. "This is the lesson that I have been leading up to. I feel now that you are all ready to at least have a go." Jura started to feel sick. If her other lessons had been leading up to this she could not bear to think what this was going to involve. What if it was worse than the terrifying lesson she had had in this bubble? She blocked that thought and tried to listen to Madame Aegrus.

"There is an enormous difference between what you think you want and what you actually want and now you must learn to switch these two around. We are all born with confused little minds and it is our job in the sel to set your mind straight – to untangle the twists you were unfortunately born with." Jura was not exactly sure where this was leading but she did not like the sound of it one bit. "What I'm trying to say," she carried on, "is that our natural responses are not always the right ones for us. They can be damaging and therefore need to be controlled. I think you've already learned a fair amount about this down here but I'm just going to take it one step further. What I'm going to say may sound a bit daunting at first but believe me, once you get the hang of it there'll be no turning back. Every fish in the ocean operates like this, so if you are to live with other fish you must be living by the same rules, understood?" All the fish in the bubble, Jura included, stared back in anticipation of what was to come.

Madame Aegrus scanned the class to check every torn-tail was paying attention. "I want you to tell yourself to say the opposite to what you instinctively want to say. For example, if you are hungry and you can see that there is not enough food for everyone, you must tell yourself that you are not hungry. You must, however, not only tell yourself this but actually make yourself believe it. I know you've learned a bit about this kind of thing already, particularly from Oprimir, but you must concentrate on it more intensely."

Jura thought this sounded ridiculous and could not understand why she would want to do that. It did not make any sense but she remembered that she must do whatever they wanted if she was to have any chance of collecting her last shell.

Madame Aegrus continued: "This will be a continual test for you all and I'm not going to say it's easy but it is the only way. If any of you are thinking you can pretend to do this and get away with it, think again. Permanent change is what we are looking for. It must become your new way of thinking. It is a way of life you must learn if you are to be accepted back into the ocean. For the duration of this test, your menfish will be staying elsewhere and will only return to you when you need to get to or from a bubble."

This new request seemed ridiculous but Jura repeated: "Blank your mind, blank your mind," over and over in her head, to keep focused on the goal of the third shell.

Madame Aegrus interrupted Jura's thoughts. "Does everyone understand what they have to do?" she bellowed across the bubble. The class was silent, feeling unsure which response would be acceptable. Then one torn-tail called out: "No."

"Oh?" replied Madame Aegrus, looking a little taken aback. "What is it that you're having trouble with?"

"Nothing, nothing at all, Madame," replied the fish, "that's why I said no, because I meant yes. That's what you said, wasn't it?"

Madame Aegrus looked at her as if she was stupid. "Yes, I said opposites but only when it's appropriate, not with questions like that, you silly torn-tail."

Now Jura really was confused. How were they supposed to know when it was appropriate to say the opposite to what they meant? This thought had obviously occurred to the others because before Jura had a chance to voice it, another torn-tail asked the very same question. "That is something you should already know," said Madame Aegrus, "and if you don't, well I guess you'll have to learn it as you go along."

When Engano came to collect Jura she decided to question him about it. "It's mainly about telling other fish what they want to hear," he said.

"I know that in lessons," replied Jura, "but in general, how am I supposed to know what other fish want to hear?"

"As Madame Aegrus probably told you, it's something you learn. You can tell by how a fish is reacting to you. He will be kinder to you if you're telling him what he wants to hear and if you're not, whether it's the truth or not, he will show his disapproval in some way," explained Engano. Jura thought back to her lesson with Oprimir where she had been told to lie and say that the sel was anything but what it actually was. She remembered how Oprimir had turned against her when she had voiced her true opinion of it. Then she remembered the first fish who had told Oprimir what she wanted to hear – that the sel was clear and fresh. He had been given second helpings of algae for saying the opposite to what he knew to be right. So she had learnt this lesson before, she knew it felt familiar.

"So I have to sense what the other fish wants to hear and tell them that, not what's actually true?" she confirmed.

"That's right," said Engano, "exactly that. It sounds difficult but once you get in the habit of it, it starts to come naturally." Jura found the idea of this not only confusing but also repellent. This revealed that her mind had not closed down as much as she had hoped, which was worrying because how could she comply with the teachers' wishes and be released?

"I'll give you a few hints," said Engano. "When

a fish asks you how you are, you always say you're fine."

"Even if I'm unhappy?" asked Jura.

"Even if your fins are hanging off, you've gone blind in one eye and your scales are bleeding. You are always fine," replied Engano. Jura had remembered telling Engano she was fine after that terrible first lesson with Madame Aegrus but only because she had not wanted to talk about it. "And you've learned that you can insult a fish by criticising where they live, haven't you? Well, that also goes for anything they like or do. Fish can be offended by the slightest sliver of truth sometimes and you will be the one who suffers if you let it slip out."

Jura realised this test would be constant, as she was often in her thinking box, minding her own business, when Oprimir, Ira or Madame Aegrus would appear and ask her how she was and question her on different subjects, monitoring how she was responding. To begin with, she was caught out a lot but she began to learn that if there was ever an opportunity in the conversation to put herself down and flatter the other fish, opposites always worked. When testing this, she tried it the other way around and didn't get any algae that night.

And so the days and nights went on and as each day passed Jura's sel education was becoming more and more complete. She was learning fast what was expected of her and the 'appropriate' answers to questions soon began to appear without much thought. A few nights without food ensured that she learned quickly. She was so thin at this point she could not afford to miss a day's food. Sometimes, fish she had not even seen before would be swimming past and would stop to ask her a question. They would always look scrawny and malnourished like the teachers in the sel generally did. From time to time a fish would bring her some food that was truly disgusting. The first time this happened she spat it out but it didn't take her long to see that was not the right reaction as she was ignored for three days afterwards. With the next lump of mud and sand she ate it gratefully to please the fish who gave it to her. It was so horrible she could hardly believe she wasn't sick but she had to abide by the rule of opposites.

In her next lesson, Madame Aegrus told them that if they responded appropriately to every question for the next five days they would be given a shell. Each torn-tail was excited by the idea of this. Some of them had not managed to collect any shells at all so they could not wait to prove themselves. Others had only one and some, like Jura, were relying on this opportunity to win their ticket to freedom.

Jura found the first four days easy. A lot of questions were about the fish who was asking so she managed to resist saying that the fish was too thin, ugly and had a wonky tail and uneven eyes, instead praising them for these flaws. On the fifth day she was asked by Madame Aegrus if she wanted to get her third shell. She paused. Was it appropriate to say yes or no? If she said yes she might risk not getting it. If she said no, Madame Aegrus might give up on her and concentrate on the other torn-tails. They stared at each other. Madame Aegrus' expression was entirely neutral – she certainly wasn't giving her any clues. Jura's future lay in the right answer. It just was not obvious like the others had been. Her thoughts rampaged through her mind. Then she remembered: "Others always first. Never think of what you want."

"Well I'm not too bothered about getting my shell," she answered suddenly. "What's more important to me is that I learn to be a better fish and learn how to behave and to be accepted." This twist of the truth had come out so smoothly she almost felt as though she meant it.

Jura looked at Madame Aegrus, eagerly awaiting her response. Had she said the right thing? Madame Aegrus did not respond at all, much to Jura's concern. In fact, she turned her tail on Jura, promptly swished it back and forth a couple of times and then disappeared into the dirty water. Jura's little heart sank. "It must have been a trick," she thought. "Now Madame Aegrus will think I don't want my shell and I won't even get any more chances to try and prove myself. I'll be down here forever…" Her sunken heart started racing. "I have to get out. I have to." Images of her bleak future flashed before her eyes. All hope had been erased by one wrongly answered question. She started shaking with the prospect of living her entire life down in the sel, in the stagnant, smelly water, never seeing any other fish again.

The fish next door to Jura noticed the state she was in. "Got one wrong, have you?" she asked, sounding rather pleased. "They've probably sussed you out. Did you really think they were ever going to give three shells to a fish whose bubbles never change colour? They set this up on purpose. Some questions are wrong whichever way you chose to answer them and I'm afraid, Miss Clear Bubbles, that was one of them. They can hardly say they won't set you free if you've got all three shells so there's only one alternative – to make sure you NEVER get them."

Jura began to feel weak. Surely what this fish was saying couldn't be true? She missed Engano. There was no one to seek reassurance from, no one even to talk to except the horrible fish next door who was only telling her things that made her feel even worse. Engano would help her out of this mess. He would talk to Lord Skumble for her. Her mind started to jump between her bubble worries, her bleak future and her longing for support from Engano. She started to feel sick. There was nothing she could do to make her bubbles change colour and she hated that. At least she could close down her mind and control her responses but her bubbles – they were beyond her control. Her frail body cowered in her thinking box, drained by the images her mind was churning up. She stared out into the darkness, a feeling of hopelessness surrounding her as thickly as the murky water she was living in.

With her vision blurred by the bleak images crowding her head, it took a few seconds for her to see that two shapes were appearing from the cloudy water. Madame Aegrus had returned and she was not alone. She and Engano stared in at Jura with smiles spread across their faces. Jura thought for a moment that her mind was playing tricks with her but no, they really were there – both of them. She looked out at them, her head so full of despair that it did not cross her mind that they could be bearing good news. Madame Aegrus spoke: "I'd like to congratulate you for reaching a stage that we consider to be worthy of release," she said. With this she lifted up her fin and there, glinting at Jura, was her third shell. Jura slowly realized that she had never been told she had answered the question wrongly. It was her who had jumped to conclusions and the fish next door who had confirmed her fears.

Madame Aegrus passed the shell to Engano. "I'll leave you both to it," she said, "Lord Skumble wishes to see you both – with the shells of course – for presentation tomorrow at noon. Until then, have a good night's sleep for tomorrow is a new beginning. Engano, settle Jura and then come and see me. We need to chat about your situation."

"I'll be with you shortly," he replied, bowing his head slightly in her direction as a sign of respect. Engano turned back to face Jura. "You've done it, you've done it, you've done it," he shouted. It was slowly beginning to sink in and as it did she turned to the jealous fish and took great pleasure in smiling from the corner of her mouth. The fish responded with only a sly look. Jura turned back to Engano. "Take it, look at it, it's yours," he said. Holding the shell heightened the reality of what was happening. She clutched it tightly, never wanting to let it go.

Jura told Engano how fearful she had been and he nestled in next to her, comforting and continually reassuring her of the brilliance of her achievement. She was so happy to see him again. As Jura began to feel sleepy Engano remembered he had to go and talk to Madame Aegrus. "Let's bury this with the others and then you can get some rest," he said. Jura reluctantly passed the shell to Engano. She knew she was going to see it again tomorrow but holding it made her feel so good. Engano dug into the sand until the other shells came into sight. "There we go," he said, placing the new one with the other two, "we'll see you three in the morning." He covered them up so neatly you would never have known there was anything there. "Right," he said, "good night, Jura, sleep well. I'll be out here until you drift off then I'll pop over to see Madame Aegrus."

Although she felt tired she was sure she wasn't going to get a wink of sleep but images of breathing properly in clearer water helped her drift off. Her dream took her into the deepest sleep she had had in the sel and when she awoke it took a few seconds for her to remember where she was. But she soon remembered. She was going today. She would be in cleaner water. She glanced out of her thinking box to see Engano waiting. As soon as he realized she was awake he was in the thinking box with her. "Come on," he said, "let's get your shells out and wipe them clean, shall we?" He began removing the sand with his tail as he had done the previous day. Back and forth it swung. Jura's eyes were fixed on the hole that was forming. Dirt sprayed out behind him creating a little mound next to the hole. Jura started to daydream. She imagined Lord Skumble's face as they showed him the shells. Would she leave straight away? How would she get back to the ocean? Perhaps she would have to go back up that tunnel. No, there must be an easier route but where that was she had no idea. Perhaps she would see Tristor again, she had almost forgotten about him. She wondered if Lord Skumble was going to tie up her tail again. She supposed he would unless of course she was going to be given a menfish there. There were so many questions rushing through her head and she could not wait to discover the answers.

Her attention was suddenly brought back when she noticed Engano had stopped for a moment. "What's going on?" she asked.

"Just having a quick breather," he replied and proceeded to carry on rather more slowly and methodically than before. He had been digging for ages now; she was sure they were not buried that deep. No, she was probably just being impatient. She was so keen to see them all that any amount of time would have felt like forever.

"Where are they?" she asked.

"Give me a minute," replied Engano, increasing the pace. Jura tried to be patient but when they still had not come into view in a few seconds later she could no longer silence her concern.

"But I can't see them," she shouted.

"Calm down," said Engano, pausing for a second. "They'll be in here, we put them here last night. I obviously haven't dug far enough down." He continued and then stopped, "then again," he said turning to Jura, "I must admit, I can't remember digging this much yesterday." He swung around to take a proper look at the hole he had dug.

"They've gone," shouted Jura, "they're not

here." Engano continued to dig but the more he dug the more Jura began to panic. "They've gone, where have they gone? My shells, someone's taken them, Engano, who's taken them? How could anyone have got in here, I was here all night. Surely I would have woken up if someone was digging up my shells? Engano, you didn't see any strange fish lurking around did you?"

"Well no," said Engano, looking deeply concerned and a little nervous, "but I'm afraid I wasn't here for much of the night. My chat with Madame Aegrus took rather longer than I thought it would."

"Engano, what are we going to do?" cried Jura.

Engano was suddenly in deep thought. "You wait here," he said, "I won't be long," and with that he swam off.

"Where are you going?" called Jura after him. His response was muted by the water.

CHAPTER 8

A decision of some urgency

Once again, Jura was left alone, her mind racing. Who had taken her shells? How had they got in? Where had Engano gone? When would he be back? Her head hurt again. Suddenly a voice interrupted her thoughts. "So it doesn't look like you're going anywhere after, all does it?" Jura looked up to see the fish next door grinning at her gleefully. She turned away. Comments like that were all she needed at a time like this. "I presume you know that Lord Skumble won't set you free until he sees your shells himself?" continued the fish.

"Just leave me alone," Jura replied, looking away. Then suddenly, Jura stared at her. "It was you wasn't it?" she said. The fish did not reply. "Of course, who else would it be? You hate me, you're jealous of me and you don't want to see me being set free. Why was it you moved thinking boxes again? What was it you said? Oh yes, you wanted to learn a thing or two. Well you haven't thought this through much, have you? Don't you think anyone is going to notice that you suddenly have all three of your shells when last night you have none and mine have mysteriously gone missing? How are you going to explain that one?" Jura felt a sudden flicker of relief. Madame Aegrus would know that this fish had stolen her shells and she would be given them back without a doubt.

"It is for that precise reason that I haven't stolen your stupid shells," responded the fish, looking down on Jura as if she was a piece of dirt on the seabed.

"Nice try," said Jura, "you've probably got another fish to take them away. I'm sure you've got some devious scheme under your fin but believe me, I'll get them back." She felt a surge of determination inside her. There was no way she was going to let this stupid, jealous fish prevent her from being set free. Jura felt less scared now and couldn't wait for Engano to return so they could start sorting things out. She stared out of her thinking box, willing him back.

A few fish swam by and as each one approached she convinced herself that it was Engano but as the hazy outline took form, it soon became obvious that it was not. Jura felt annoyed that he should disappear in her time of need; surely he knew she would need him more than ever now? But she also felt concerned. What was keeping him? The more time passed, the harder it was to ignore the neighbouring fish, who was hoping Engano's disappearing act had a sinister explanation.

Minutes turned to hours. Jura's body was tense and her head drained from exhausting all possible options in her mind. Night fell and all the other menfish were in their usual spots outside the cage of their torntails. Jura stayed wide-eyed and expectant all night. So eager was she not to miss Engano's return, she hardly dared blink. Hour upon weary hour faded painfully behind her and still no Engano. She found it difficult not to worry that he was being blamed for not protecting her shells well enough. But if that was the case, surely Madame Aegrus was as much to blame? She was the one who had called him away, after all.

As morning arrived, Jura's eyes were stinging and whatever energy she had been holding on to had vanished. Engano had never disappeared like this during the whole time she had known him. A sudden urge came over her to shout his name although she knew it was pointless. The dense water would prevent any call being heard. As her call hit the unyielding water and dissolved, a deep heaviness swelled within her. The continual drone of her thoughts was beginning to madden her.

Her mind was so preoccupied that she hadn't even noticed that the rest of the fish had gone to learn their lessons that morning. Initially, she was relieved, as the smug presence next door was no longer. Then suddenly she felt stupid; why hadn't she asked another fish if they knew what was going on? The thought had not even entered her mind, she had been intent on working it out herself. Hope was all she had to rely on. Hope that this actually had an obvious explanation that she had overlooked.

Time continued, as it does, and Jura's head began to feel numb. Her thoughts had packed up and left, angry at being trapped and squashed together. Her blurred eyes snapped back into focus by the emergence of a shoal of pink, wiggling forms. The shrimps had returned and Jura felt deeply grateful for their presence. She had not seen them for a long time and although they were deaf and couldn't help her, she remembered the relaxing effect they had had on her previously.

Just as she was pondering on the pointless nature of cleaning a place that remained resolutely dirty, she heard a voice: "I'm afraid he won't be coming back," it said. Jura almost jumped out of her thinking box. The words floated through the water, unaffected by the dirt. They had a soft, melodious quality and Jura thought for a second that perhaps she had imagined them.

"Who said that?" she asked, expecting a fish to emerge from the haze.

"I did," came the voice. Jura's eyes strained to see the owner of this mysterious voice. "Right here," came the voice. Jura refocused to see a shrimp directly in front of her.

"You?" she exclaimed, feeling highly confused, "but you're d…"

"Dead-heads?" interrupted the shrimp. "Quite the opposite, as is everything you see down here. Things aren't as they appear, Jura. They haven't been teaching you about opposites for nothing. Their plan is that things down here will slowly appear more normal. You must be set free before the true danger begins."

Jura's mind began to somersault again. "They are never planning on releasing you, Engano included, I'm afraid. The dark forces are stronger than you'd ever believe and deceit is the key to success down here. To you, it has been unpleasant but temporary, for them, the beginning of a growing undersea empire."

Jura looked at the shrimp suspiciously. Her musical voice continued. "It is Engano who stole your shells, Jura – none other than your trusted menfish." The words, although spoken with such softness and grace, hit Jura like a brick.

"What are you talking about and who are you anyway?" snapped Jura defensively. The shrimp's calm manner did not flicker even for a second.

"Us shrimps or 'dead-heads' as they believe down here, are from the real ocean," she continued.

"I never saw you there," Jura replied, doubtfully.

"That's probably because you've never been there," said the shrimp, looking deeply in her eyes. It was as if the shrimp could see something that she was not aware she was showing.

"I was born there, thank you very much," responded Jura indignantly, "under the rule of the King and Queen."

"And that's where you hope to return to, is it?" said the shrimp.

"Well, it's better than here, isn't it?" replied Jura.

"Marginally, I dare say," the shrimp went on, "but dear Jura, there is so much more to the ocean and I think you know this too – or you did at one time anyway." The shrimp's melodic voice had an almost magnetic quality that made her listen through no apparent choice of her own.

"Can you remember why you were actually sent down here, Jura?" said the shrimp, suddenly looking very serious. It all seemed so long ago. As Jura found the memory, the shrimp continued. "You knew there was more food higher up in the ocean as soon as you were born. You should never have been punished for that and certainly wouldn't have been at one time but things are not the same down here anymore. Corrupt minds are breeding and the sel is becoming a threat to the livelihood of the whole ocean."

Jura had a sudden thought. "Why should I believe you more than Engano?" she said. "He's been my loyal friend for the whole time I've been here, which let's face it, is most of my life. I don't know one thing about you and to be honest I'd prefer to wait for Engano. He'll be back, you'll see," she said with a confidence she didn't feel.

"I wouldn't be so sure about that," said the shrimp.

"Oh wouldn't you?" snapped Jura. "Who knows him better, you or me? I think we both know the answer to that." The shrimp was scaring Jura and she did not want to hear what she was saying. She had the plan in her head. Engano was going to return, she would tell him about the thieving fish next door and her shells would be returned. She would be released and that would be that. End of sel.

"Believe what you like," said the shrimp. "I know there is no reason for you to trust me but if you can remember how you once knew there was more food above then that may help you to believe me."

"Just leave me will you?" cried Jura, "I need to see Engano."

"Jura," said the shrimp calmly, "I'm not forcing you to come with me; the decision is entirely yours. I'm merely giving you an option out of here but please hear what I have to say."

"I've heard," said Jura firmly, "and I want to wait for Engano."

"You've heard only the beginning," said the shrimp, "and if you'd allow me to expand on it a little I'd be most grateful."

Jura's eyes were drawn back to the shrimp's and something inside her chose to listen. "Well, I suppose I've got nothing else to do while I wait for Engano," she said, "go on then."

The shrimp smiled softly. "I don't wish to frighten you, Jura," she continued, "but the truth about the sel is far from pleasant."

"I know what it's like down here," replied Jura. "I've lived here and I know it's hardly a place I'd chose to live but today is the day I'm being set free and I'm not risking that for anyone."

"Stay here if you wish," said the shrimp "but hear me out first." Jura looked suspiciously into the shrimp's eyes. "I know it seems Engano cares for you and I'm sure if he could, he would," the shrimp carried on, "but he is under the claws of Lord Skumble. They all are, Jura – every menfish down here. Their intentions may appear to be good but in the sel there is no such thing. Lord Skumble is trying to take over the ocean. He's dangerous, Jura and must be stopped. Many are beyond the point where they can escape but you are not one of these fish."

Jura stared at the shrimp questioningly. "You know this," the shrimp continued "for you've feared this being a reason for them keeping you." The shrimp paused. "Your bubbles," she said. "It is certainly not merely by an act of chance that they do not change colour. You have never totally crushed yourself to please them or your bubbles would have changed. You sensed this would threaten them and indeed it did. Jura, it is at this point that you are in the greatest danger. The shells you have collected are not tickets to freedom. They are the very opposite. They are purely for the benefit of Lord Skumble. In his eyes, to have collected three shells is evidence that you are now ready to be a menfish. After you've proved yourself in this role you become a teacher. Rewards are reaped for following this path – or so they seem to be anyway – but the fish that grow old down here slowly become engulfed by the darkness that surrounds them. Menfish are merely torn-tails who've been awarded their shells. When Lord Skumble receives your shells your tail will be mended but believe me, the price you will have to pay for it is one too terrible for many ears."

Jura twitched awkwardly inside but she was intrigued now and had to hear more. "In exchange for your tail, Lord Skumble steals something a lot more precious from you." The shrimp's eyes moved to and fro uncomfortably.

Jura watched them intently. "What?" she cried urgently.

The shrimp's eyes rested on Jura again, saddened by what she was about to say. "Jura, in return for your tail, Lord Skumble takes from you your desire to leave." Jura's scales prickled. "Tristor," continued the shrimp, "is a perfect example of this. They all are, in fact, teachers and menfish alike and I think you'll agree when I say that their withered forms betray this somewhat. Engano is relatively new to his role and that is why he doesn't look as bad as most. I drew your attention to Tristor for his form shows the loss more clearly than any other, I feel. This is because he, like you, once knew. He chose not to remember that, however, and the result could hardly be clearer. I talked to Tristor as a torn-tail but his ears had already closed. Now, although so much of his sweet nature remains, his desire to escape has dissolved so much that Lord Skumble allows him to swim to the entrance safe in the knowledge that he will never leave. He could be commanded to leave the sel entirely and he would still return."

Jura was suddenly interrupted by another thought that entered her head and she promptly voiced it. "If what you say is true," she said, "then why have my shells been stolen? Why has Engano taken them?" The shrimp paused and cast her eyes down; she looked troubled by what she was about to say.

"He's taken them to Lord Skumble," she said eventually.

"But why? Why didn't he just wait and take

them with me and why did he pretend he didn't know where they were? This doesn't make sense."

"I don't want to have to tell you so much at once for the truth is painful even to an outsider's ear but if it helps you to understand, I feel I must. Engano took your shells for one reason," said the shrimp, pausing again.

"Just tell me," cried Jura impatiently.

"To frighten you," said the shrimp. "He was starting off the process for Lord Skumble."

"What do you mean?" asked Jura.

"Lord Skumble can only eliminate your desire to leave when your mind is fearful. By stealing your shells and disappearing like he did, Engano was ensuring that your state of fear is complete. Before long, Lord Skumble will arrive here and his ploy will begin."

Jura was speechless. What was she to think? "I'll say it again, Jura, for it concerns me greatly," said the shrimp, "my purpose is not to frighten you, although it may seem that way. I could see no other way than to tell you the truth and I could not lie to you and pretend that it would be in any way pleasant. I only wish I could have told you more slowly but it seems circumstances would not allow it. It's clear that you are strong enough to hear this otherwise it wouldn't have happened this way."

Jura felt anything but strong at this moment and felt unsure who or what to believe. Although what the shrimp was saying was truly horrifying, her presence calmed her. She recalled the effect the shrimps had had on her when she'd watched them with Engano, believing them to be dead-heads. Part of her wanted to reject what the shrimp was saying and continue waiting for Engano, after all, she had only just met this mysterious creature. But she knew that ignoring the shrimp's words was too great a risk. A vivid image of Tristor reinforced this. She could not afford to risk ending up like him.

Just then, a claw appeared out of the cloudy water. One claw was enough for Jura and she leapt towards the shrimp. In a flash, she was out of her thinking box and the shrimp was pulling her along at a speed she would not have believed she was capable of. She glanced behind her and met a pair of beady eyes: Lord Skumble's, and they were red with anger. His black claws were churning up clouds of sand as he rampaged through the sel after them. The sight of him, although terrifying, was at least a sign to Jura that she had made the right decision. Jura clung to the shrimp, hardly daring to look behind them. Even without looking, she could feel Lord Skumble's dark shape gaining on them.

From what Jura could work out, they seemed to be heading in the opposite direction from where she arrived in the sel. She presumed the shrimp knew where she was taking her. This was certainly no time for questions. They seemed to be heading into thicker and thicker water and Jura could not understand how the shrimp was still managing to dart through it. It did not seem to be tiring at all, which was just as well for neither was Lord Skumble. In fact, he seemed to be in his element as the water became cloudier and he was catching them up. Jura dared to glance behind once more but shouldn't have as he was now close enough to smell her fear and as he did he was propelled on by its essence. His claws were moving so fast they were blurring into one sharp weapon, eager to be put to use. The more Jura looked at Lord Skumble, the closer he got. She had to look ahead, she knew she must. She could feel his eyes trying to pierce into her and pull her towards him; she must resist it. But the closer he got, the harder she found it not to look. The shrimp sensed Jura's predicament. "Don't look back," she shouted. "Whatever you do, stay focused ahead of you." Jura pulled her eyes forward and as she did, their path changed.

Their surroundings seemed to be closing in on them. She could not see exactly what it was that gave her that feeling for the water was too thick. As she strained her eyes, she suddenly became aware that they were in a tunnel. It certainly was not the same one she had arrived in the sel through. It was about three times as wide and a little lighter too. They darted through it. Then, with no warning the tunnel began to bend wildly to the left and right. Back and forth, back and forth, relentlessly. Fortunately, the shrimp seemed to know exactly where it was going, to Jura's relief. Left to her own devices, she would have stood no chance.

Jura hoped the tunnel would straighten out again soon as it was beginning to make her feel dizzy. Not only did it continue to twist and turn most awkwardly but the water started to change. Jura had felt a current before when she was on her way down to the sel but it hadn't been anything like this one. Its force was gathering up and soon became unlike anything Jura had ever felt. It churned up the seabed and smashed against the sides of the tunnel, breaking on them and sending them spiralling along. Jura clung on with all her might. She must not lose the shrimp – she was her only hope. The current seemed to be increasing the further through the tunnel they went. It threw them about as if they were grains of sand. Jura could not focus anymore. She had no idea which way they were facing. The force of the water continued to increase and they were hurled into the side of the tunnel. Jura's skin was scraped but she felt so terrified she barely felt it. Crash! The water had picked them up and thrown them against the opposite side. It felt like they were caught in a whirlpool. Thump! She was propelled into the side, her tail lashing round for its share of the pain. She could see no way out of this situation. The water, it seemed, wanted their lives and she was beginning to feel that she would have no option but to succumb. Its strength demanded every part of her to fight for survival against it. The harder she fought, the stronger it was becoming until suddenly they jerked to a halt.

    The water had not relented but they had certainly stopped. When she had managed to gather her mind enough, she realized that they had been caught by something. It had wound itself around them and they were locked in its grasp. They were being held absolutely still in the raging waters; their captor was certainly not taking any chances. It was neither hard nor soft, almost rubbery; a strange texture, Jura thought, one she had not come across before. They were being squeezed so tightly that the wild waters could not even sway them. It was gushing past them at such a rate that seeing proved to be an impossibility, in fact all their senses had been impaired by their surroundings. It was as though everything had been on fast-forward – themselves included – and then, bang! They had been paused but nothing else had. It was a curious sensation to be static when all around you is in furious turmoil.

After a few long seconds, their captor began to move slowly upwards, taking them with it. Jura wanted to talk to the shrimp but knew there was no way she could in the raging waters. They seemed no challenge at all for their captor, though, whose strength was unimaginable.

Up and up they were taken, and although it was gradual, Jura slowly began to feel the strength of the water beginning to wane. As they rose higher still, the water was not only calming down considerably but it also seemed to be becoming clearer. Where they were being taken, Jura had no idea but whatever lay ahead could surely not be worse than what they had just left behind them.

Just as she was noticing that her surroundings were starting to improve, their speed increased until it felt like they were moving through the paused ocean. In a sudden burst, they arrived face to face with a rather large creature like no other Jura had seen before in her life.

CHAPTER 9

Octalma, Octrus and the octopi

Fish of all shapes, sizes and colours darted to and fro, each with their own business. And there was not a torn-tail or menfish in sight. Jura blinked several times to check that she was actually seeing this. Her eyes confirmed that it was real just as a shriek from the shrimp reminded her that her hearing was intact. The creature's clasp had released and a smile was beaming at them from a large, round face. The shrimp's excitement was surging through the water in all directions. Jura felt it so strongly the water itself was tingling. "Sereno," cried the creature, "good to see you again, my friend. I was beginning to wonder. Rumours have reached us that danger is increasing in the sel and by the look of it, these rumours bear the truth."

Oceans Apart

The shrimp looked up at the creature. "I would like to thank you most sincerely, my favourite octopus," she said, "for without your help I doubt whether I would have escaped this time."

"What are you saying?" responded the octopus. "I merely lent you a tentacle – God knows I have enough of them," and with that, she swung around seven other tentacles, reinforcing her statement. "You would have found your own way without me, Sereno, I just speeded up the procedure a little."

"Well, whatever the outcome may have been, we shall never know but I am most grateful to you, Octalma, all the same," replied Sereno.

"This must be Jura," said Octalma, beaming down at her. "Congratulations," she said. "It hasn't been easy for you, I know, but you can believe me when I say you made the right decision to listen to Sereno. The shrimps are gems in the ocean. You wouldn't see me offering to live in the sel for the benefit of fish I didn't even know." She turned to the shrimp. "It's a remarkable thing, Sereno, and I'm truly proud of you."

Sereno blushed a darker shade of pink, smiled and then turned serious. "Once you've seen the extent of what's happening down there, Octalma, you can't ignore it. The more fish Lord Skumble darkens, the bigger the threat to the entire ocean. It cannot and will not be allowed to happen if I have anything to do with it and it is for that reason that I must return." Jura twitched. "Not quite yet, Jura, don't worry, but it is my duty and you are safe here. It is safer than anywhere you have known so far in your life."

"Let me take you both to my house," said Octalma. "You must be exhausted after such an ordeal." She wrapped them both up in one of her long tentacles again and carried them gently through the water. As they moved, Jura became aware that the temperature of the water had risen and she could relax as it was no longer so bitterly cold that her body tensed itself in the hope of trapping some warmth. Jura's adventure had worn her out. She felt her mind had been everywhere it was capable of in the last couple of days. Her new environment, although strange, felt easier. Already she could feel that there were fewer demands on her here. As the octopus bobbed through the water, the movement gently rocked Jura to sleep and she was carried away from her thoughts and into her dreams.

She awoke hours later feeling a little dazed. As she opened her eyes, they met a mass of tentacles that were twisting and turning. They appeared to be making something out of reeds and with so many of them on the job it looked no effort at all. In and out, up and down the reeds were being wound. "Ah," cried Octalma, noticing Jura was awake, "welcome," she said. Jura's eyes looked up from the entanglement of tentacles. "Before I fetch you something to eat I would like to introduce you to my family. This is Octrus," she said pointing towards a large, thick-tentacled, wise-looking octopus. He did not speak but nodded in Jura's direction, he seemed friendly but preoccupied. His eyes looked like they had seen a lot in their time and were greying slightly because of it. His tentacles moved slowly and he worked methodically. Jura felt comfortable in his quiet presence for despite his rather detached demeanour, he wasn't in the least bit threatening.

Beside Octrus were two small octopi. "These are our little ones," said Octalma proudly. "This is Octi and this is Octula." The octopi seemed to be bursting with energy. They were young, eager-eyed, soft-faced, nimble-tentacled octa-babies.

"Hello, Jura," they squealed in synchrony, their fresh, excited faces delighting Jura. There seemed to be so much hope in their eyes unlike Octrus', where hope had once lived but no longer felt safe to stay.

As Jura took in her new surroundings, Octalma busily prepared some breakfast for her. Jura noticed she was in a house made from hundreds of different types of reeds. She didn't know that so many different kinds even existed. There were greens of every shade imaginable. Some were smooth, some jagged, some thin, some thick, some soft and shiny, some rough and spiky. They had all been wound together to make a house just big enough to accommodate all four of them. There was not a lot of room for movement when they were all in there. She supposed that was why they were still busy building. There was a small door directly ahead of Jura that barely looked big enough for Octrus to fit through. It was round and was draped with loose reeds hanging down like a curtain.

Octalma appeared from the corner of the house, tentacles laden with succulent, fresh algae. Jura's eyes widened and she felt a bolt of hunger shoot through her body. Octalma poured the algae out in front of Jura and she gobbled it up hungrily. As she began to eat, the first few mouthfuls reminded her how hungry she was. She had exerted all her energy the previous day without even a morsel to sustain her. She had been running on pure adrenalin. Now she had relaxed a little, her appetite had returned and she revelled in satisfying it. On swallowing her final mouthful her mind seemed suddenly to be taken to Sereno. As if answering her thought, Octalma's voice broke through it. "Sereno has just gone for a little swim – she won't be long. I know you must be eager to see her, there must be a lot you want to ask her." Jura did not answer, she simply smiled in response.

The octopi seemed excited by their guest and kept looking over at Jura playfully. She felt they wanted her to play with them but they knew they had a job to do. "Come on, you two," said Octalma, noticing their distraction. "This won't take long and then you can play."

Jura's eyes were drawn away from them suddenly by the emergence of Sereno. She appeared through the reed curtain and swam over to Jura. "How are you feeling this morning?" she asked in her calming melodic voice. That was a good question and Jura wasn't entirely sure of the answer.

"I'm fine," she responded out of habit.

"Let's go for a swim," said Sereno and with that she pulled a reed up and was about to wrap it around Jura's tail but as Jura felt the reed touch her she flinched nervously and pulled away. The memory of her entrance into the sel flashed before her eyes, filling her with fear. What if this was all another trick?

Her wits sprung about her like armed bodyguards.

"What are you doing to me?" she shouted at Sereno. The octopi were startled by this sudden change of mood and looked over to see what had caused it. Sereno was initially shocked by such a reaction too but suddenly realized what was going on.

"It's happened before?" she asked. Jura nodded, her eyes glazing over. "Listen, Jura," she said, "whatever happened to you down there will not repeat itself unless you choose to return. Now you've got yourself this far I very much doubt that you will but the option is always going to be there if you want it. Nothing or no one however can force you to return against your will."

Jura looked at Sereno apprehensively. "How do I know that you're telling me the truth?" she asked, a little shaken.

"The answer is, you don't," said Sereno. "Rely on your instincts, Jura, for they know the answers. I can tell you all I know but it is you who must make your decisions and not me. I can offer you guidance though, and that I will, but really that's all I can do."

Sereno seemed to be sincere but Jura still felt very wary. She eventually concluded that being able to swim couldn't do her any harm but she certainly wasn't going to be lured down any more tunnels. "Okay," Jura said at last, "you can wrap that reed around my tail but next time just tell me first what you're doing." Sereno apologized and before long the two of them were swimming out of the door together.

The water was so much cleaner up here and there was an abundance of algae. If she had wanted to she could have filled her stomach in a matter of seconds; she would never get hungry here. Seeing so much food readily available was an exciting novelty. Overwhelmed by the simplicity of finding it she ate a little although she was not hungry in the least. And there was such a variety of fish here it felt like a treat for Jura's eyes to watch them float past. None of them seemed perturbed by Sereno and Jura's presence. They all seemed to have a similar look of deep concentration in their eyes.

Before long, Sereno stopped in the water and turned to face Jura. "I have something for you," she said with a serious tone. "Something you have earned simply by allowing me to bring you here." Jura was intrigued. Sereno reached behind her and pulled something out from the curl of her tail. A bright twinkle reflected in Jura's eyes. She winced and then quickly refocused. Sereno was holding a tiny, round, ivory-coloured ball that shone as brightly as a star. Silver threads of light reflected off it in all directions, bouncing off the water and heading to unknown places. As Jura looked at it she felt a warm sensation surge through her, relaxing every cell in her body. The light from it seemed to cover her in a misty glow. The feeling was so intense it was overwhelming. Sereno waited until Jura was ready and then gently handed it to her. She accepted it cautiously. "Keep this pearl with you, Jura, and guard it with your life, for it will protect you so long as you do not allow possession of it by another. As long as it is with you, you can come to no harm. Hand it over and trouble will undoubtedly arise. Lord Skumble is aware that you have it and may try to get it from you but it is yours, Jura, and allowing anyone to take it, particularly Lord Skumble, will mean disaster." Jura looked at the pearl, a little daunted by the responsibility of it but also relieved. Something about it comforted her greatly for reasons she could not articulate. She tucked it under her fin and could feel it tingling against her scales.

Sereno continued: "Lord Skumble's powers are becoming greater than even I am aware of," she said. "I've taken that route many a time and never has such a thing happened. Lord Skumble was controlling that water. His powers have never stretched that far before and it concerns me. He'll do what he can to pull fish down from above. He rises to the challenge quite wholeheartedly, in fact."

"But why would I want to go back to the sel?" asked Jura. "I've spent most of my life collecting shells so I would be set free, or so I thought at the time anyway."

"As I said," continued Sereno, "keep hold of your pearl and you'll have no problems, lose it and the pull will be greater than you could anticipate." Jura wasn't entirely sure what Sereno meant. "Remember the choice is always yours, even when it may appear that it is not. You are the one who decides which direction looks the most inviting. Remember when you wondered if there was more food higher up in the ocean? This is what you were sensing. You saw how concerned the King and Queen were at the mere suggestion of a fish moving higher up. They are equally determined to bring the ones down from above." Jura was starting to feel that perhaps nowhere was safe.

"It doesn't have to be anything to fear, Jura. In fact, if you keep your pearl with you, its very essence will protect you," finished Sereno.

This all seemed a bit strange to Jura's ears. "I understand," she heard coming from her mouth, even though she didn't.

"Do you really?" asked Sereno, "because it isn't something you should know, given your circumstances. Things like this take time to understand." Jura suddenly felt a flash of embarrassment. She had become so used to talking in opposites in the sel that she found her instinctive response was now one she did not mean at all. Now this was being questioned she felt nervous. It had taken so long for her to adjust her mind in the sel and now she had, the last thing she wanted was to have to change again.

"Yes I do understand," she replied in a tone that clearly communicated to Sereno that this was a delicate matter. Sereno wisely did not respond. Any response would have provoked an eruption in Jura at that moment.

They swam on together, both deep in thought. Sereno was concerned by Jura's reaction. She knew from past experience what a difficult task it was to recover from being in the sel, even with a helping hand. She lived in hope of seeing a smooth transition but deep down wasn't entirely sure if it was possible. She would have to tread carefully, as always.

Jura's mind was in turmoil and unfortunately this was causing her to question Sereno's integrity. She thought back to Engano; had she made the right choice by leaving him? Perhaps he really was going to set her free. Maybe now she had complicated matters even more by following Sereno. But it was so much cleaner up here… And the pearl…

They swam through the water, swerving in and out of the kelp, seaweed and reeds. They passed some very strange-looking fish. The flat ones amused Jura at first until she wondered if there were creatures here that were capable of squashing you flat. Jura shivered from her bones to her scales at the mere thought and propelled herself a little faster, suddenly imagining that such a creature was behind them.

They saw some fish 10 times Jura's size and as they drifted past she was careful to avoid eye contact, just in case. As they were swimming towards a large clump of pale-green seaweed Jura noticed another torn-tail coming towards them, being guided by a shrimp. "Rio," called Sereno to the shrimp. Rio smiled broadly and stopped to talk to Sereno. Jura looked at the other torn-tail, who looked sad, confused and even a little lost. She smiled but he looked away awkwardly and they swam on. This unnerved Jura further still.

"Why do the fish here act so strangely?" she asked Sereno. "They all seem so preoccupied. Is there something I should know about this place?"

Sereno moved closer to Jura and spoke quietly. "The fish here are learning things that aren't altogether easy, Jura," she said. "They are learning to change." Jura looked at Sereno suspiciously. She was reminded of the lessons in the sel. She remembered Madame Aegrus telling them that they had to change the way they were thinking. Was it all happening again? She couldn't, not again.

"What kind of change?" Jura asked nervously.

"Change concerning the ocean both in the widest sense of the word and the smallest," Sereno said.

"Smallest?" echoed Jura.

"Smallest meaning you," said Sereno. Jura looked at her questioningly. "Each individual fish," continued Sereno. "No fish can be expected to take on the entire ocean but as each fish changes, so the ocean will as a whole."

"What if I don't want to change anymore?" asked Jura.

"Then you will probably be more comfortable in the sel," responded Sereno, not unkindly.

This did not make any sense to Jura. "In the sel I was being forced to change the whole time I was living there," she said, "and that's what I didn't like. Now I'm out, I don't want to change anymore."

Sereno paused. "My idea of change is very different from Lord Skumble's," she said. "If you are comfortable with his way then you can return at any time, but if I'm not mistaken, I think you know that the changes in the sel weren't for your benefit. Here, however, I can assure you they are and you will appreciate that so long as you don't allow your experience in the sel to darken the eyes you look from."

Jura felt a little overwhelmed. Sereno noticed and suggested they turn back. "You probably haven't swum as far as this for a long time," she said. Jura could barely even remember the last time she had swum on her own. Now she came to think of it, she had never swum that far – never in her whole life. That had to count for something.

By the time they reached Octalma's house again, Jura's little fins were feeling weak and weary. She was relieved to be back and to see the octopi again. The feeling was evidently mutual as the moment they saw Jura's head appear through the reed curtain they were squabbling over which tentacle was going to pull her in. When they saw that she was quite capable of entering on her own accord they were rather put out. They wanted to befriend her but weren't altogether sure how. Jura's mind felt burdened. She did not like the idea of having to change again at all.

The octopi were deeply anxious to impress their new lodger and were twisting and contorting their tentacles to see who could make the funniest shape out of themselves. It was a relief for Jura to watch them. They appeared not to have a care in the world; all that mattered was that moment. She watched them giggling, twisting and turning and for a moment let go of her heavy thoughts and was drawn into their world of uncomplicated contentment.

For the next few days, Sereno thought a lot about Jura's situation. She eventually concluded that she must tell her everything. She invited Jura for a swim with her. Jura did not realize that continuing to live in her sel mindset could not be an option here. In fact, since her chat with Sereno about changing, she had been convincing herself that it wasn't really necessary. She told herself that if it was important, Sereno would have told her more about it by now.

Their swim began in silence. After a few minutes, Sereno knew she must speak to Jura. "Do you know why I wanted to go for a swim with you today?" she asked. Although Jura was beginning to suspect she did, she played safe.

"No idea," she replied.

"Do you remember our last conversation?" asked Sereno.

"Not really," Jura lied.

"This is your home now," continued Sereno. "There are things here for you to learn. You are a strong fish, Jura, I have no doubt about that and I sense you'll go far. I, however, have different tasks to fulfil. I'm afraid my time has come to return to the sel. As much as I would love to stay, my destiny is clear. The destruction is too great in the sel and I must do all I can to help turn it around. My part may seem small when compared to the power of Lord Skumble yet, as I have said before, with each fish that is shown another way, the ocean will have a better chance of being restored to the peaceful state it once lived in.

"But you can't go back," cried Jura. "You felt the power of that water and Lord Skumble will know it was you who was rescuing me. He'll be after you the moment he sees your face down there. Stay here where you're safe."

Sereno looked kindly at Jura. "My dear Jura," she said, "these worries are not for you. They will be taken care of."

"But how? He'll get you, I saw those angry eyes, you'll never get away with it – don't go."

As Jura began to panic, the pearl seemed to be slipping from her grasp. Until now it had been nestled under her fin. In fact, it was so comfortable there she had almost forgotten that she had it. She tried half-heartedly to pull it back but her mind was concentrating on Sereno's news. The more worked up Jura became, the more intent the pearl became on escaping. A wave of panic flooded through her as the pearl slipped further still and she began to notice that the water was thickening around her. "He'll imprison you or worse, Sereno, you can't go back." Her oxygen intake began to feel restricted, her whole body was becoming stressed and as she envisaged the bleak future she had conjured up for Sereno, her environment seemed to change further still. It was slowly beginning to resemble the sel. Perhaps it had all been an illusion. Perhaps she was still there and this other place had been a figment of her imagination. The further her mind hurtled in this direction the thicker the water grew until as far as she could tell, she was in the sel. It was real at this moment and the place where she was physically did not exist, could not exist. She saw what her mind saw and her worst fears had come to life before her eyes. As Jura struggled both physically and mentally, Sereno could tell that Jura had gone elsewhere by a cloudiness that had veiled her eyes and the fact that the pearl was no longer with her.

CHAPTER 10
A matter of choice

As Jura believed she was back in the sel, so she was, but just as Engano caught sight of her something inside her flickered. For a split moment her mind saw what she was doing. It was like a flash of light had struck her eyes, as if in warning. The light had caused them to change focus momentarily and with a jolt of adrenalin she remembered her escape from the sel, bringing her back to the present. As her mind gradually returned, her eyes focused once again, the pearl crept back under her fin and the water slowly cleared.

She blinked several times. She felt as if something had entered her head and sucked out every morsel of energy. The feeling had been so intense she could not remember what had triggered it. She stared out ahead of her trying to recall what had led her mind down there. Everything appeared to be hazy and her head felt like she had just swum full speed into a wall.

"I'll be fine," said Sereno finally but Jura stared at her blankly. It was as if every thought in her head had been erased. "Don't worry," continued Sereno, unaware of the extent to which Jura had vacated.

"About what?" asked Jura, feeling a little ashamed. She knew she had known what Sereno was talking about but had lost the thread.

"The sel," said Sereno, beginning to feel more concerned than she was letting on. "I'm going to be okay there. I think you were scared about what would happen to you if you returned, not me. I will be protected, Jura. It may be difficult but I must return. You, on the other hand, must learn not to return."

Jura looked at Sereno inquisitively. Did she know where she had just been? "Correct me if I'm mistaken," Sereno continued, "but I recognize that cloudy look." Jura felt tense suddenly. "As I've said before, you will always have the option to return but it's a dangerous habit. By allowing the force to pull you down, you are doubling its power. With its strength and yours combined you have little hope. Lord Skumble's empire is fuelled by the energy of those who succumb to the fears and rules of the sel. He has a fast-growing collection of pearls down there and is constantly on the search for more. Your task here is to keep hold of yours, for letting it go will threaten not only your survival but also that of the ocean. Even when it feels the least of your concerns,

Jura, believe me when I tell you that when you let it go, nothing else can work. You may not be in the sel anymore but as you've seen, your mind is free to wander where it chooses. Your physical whereabouts are not nearly of such concern to Lord Skumble as your pearl. Once you learn to keep it with you, you'll sever the link with him. Only when that has been achieved can you really be free from the sel. It is no easy task, Jura, and I couldn't pretend to you that it is. It is what you are sensing all around you here. The looks of concentration on the faces of the fish are because of this. Every fish here is aware of the responsibility they have in the future of the ocean. They are constantly fighting a battle with the pearl that they have been given, resisting the pull from Lord Skumble. Some are drawn down to the sel, unable to resist the force that's taking their pearl away from them and towards him. Others stay and have to watch their friends descend. Many are here struggling against him and some are out of Lord Skumble's reach now, they have chosen to cut the link."

Jura listened in silence. She was feeling rather daunted by this place. She wasn't sure she liked the idea of such responsibility. She was glad, however, that Sereno had clarified a few things for her. She knew there was something a little ominous going on here and although she was surprised at the explanation, at least it accounted for the atmosphere.

Jura had hoped everything would be easy now. She'd been rescued and left her past behind. How strange it was so discover that things were not solely black and white. There were hundreds of colours in between. "You cannot be rescued from the sel and leave it behind you without an immensely strong mind," Sereno continued. "Many fish believe that being rescued is the end of the sel. How can it be this way? It makes no sense to rely on another fish to find your freedom for you. Another fish can guide you like I have but I can only bring you here and you must do the rest alone."

"Alone?" cried Jura, "but I can't".

"Well, not entirely alone at this stage," said Sereno. "You have your pearl and if you allow it to, it will guide you in the right direction."

"Octalma and Octrus have warmed to you. They say you are very welcome to stay with them but to understand that they too are busy." Jura felt relieved to hear that she had somewhere to go, somewhere she could call her home, if only temporarily. "I will be leaving here tomorrow, Jura. Try not to fear for me as it can only hinder both of us. When or even if we will meet again I cannot say, that must be left for the ocean to decide." Jura felt frightened by this news. She wanted her to stay but knew she had to let her go. She liked having Sereno with her; although she had not known her for long she felt safe around her now. When Sereno had gone it would be up to Jura to choose wisely and the idea of that was unnerving.

They both swam on in silence for a short while. Jura needed time to absorb it all. As it sunk in, she started to worry again. Sereno sensed this and before she took a downward spiral she managed to soothe her. She talked to Jura as if she was a child of her own, reassuring her and listening to her. She did not judge her for panicking about the change as she knew it could be very frightening.

At last they returned to Octalma's house, both fatigued for their own reasons. Jura felt too tired to worry any more about the consequences of what she had learnt that day. That night they ate a hearty meal with Octalma, Octrus and the octopi. The algae and plankton that Octalma served was prepared in the most delicious way. She had pressed little balls of algae together, mixed with thin strips of seaweed, wrapped each one up in a reed and left them to set for a few days. The result of this maturation process was a juicy combination of both sweet and savoury which their taste buds relished. Overwhelmed by such delicious food, Jura gobbled up a few more than she needed and with both stomach and mind full to bursting, her sleep came to summon her earlier than usual that night. She tried to resist it, knowing that Sereno was leaving the following day, but couldn't help but submit. From time to time during the night, Jura awoke from her dreams to a feeling of heaviness pulling at her. Without the strength of mind or body to understand it, she chose to accept the help sleep was offering and return to its cosy chamber.

When morning arrived, Jura at least felt physically refreshed if nothing more. The atmosphere in the house was one of unspoken fear. Sereno's mission was concerning even for Octalma and Octrus, although they knew too well the importance of it. They were aware that it had to be done but at the same time wished it could be someone they did not know who had been born with this responsibility.

Oceans Apart

They admired Sereno greatly though and tried to keep their spirits raised if only for her sake. Sereno seemed focused; she knew what was ahead but she had done it before and she would do it again. It may not have held such a high risk for her previously but she was an intelligent shrimp and was aware of the strength of her powers.

There was a gentle current in the ocean that morning guiding Sereno in the direction she had to take. She was not keen on long goodbyes; she never felt they were necessary. "If we are to meet again we shall and if not, that's how it must be," she said. "Goodbye and good luck to you all," and she was gone.

Sereno's departure was difficult for Jura. She retreated into the corner, feeling sorry for herself. The little octopi did not even try to cheer her up. They sensed she wasn't in the mood for jokes and they were right. Octalma floated over to her and wrapped a long tentacle around her. "I know it's not easy," she said, "but you're here now. Sereno has shown you this place and it is up to you what you make of it. It's not a bad place to be, demanding maybe but you're not trapped like you were in the sel."

"Things just seem so complicated," sobbed Jura. "All I ever wanted was to be allowed to live; I didn't want anything more than that."

"I know," said Octalma, "it seems that's what we all want but unfortunately there are forces that are working to the contrary and to keep our lives we must resist them."

"How long have you lived here?" asked Jura.

"All my life," replied Octalma. "I was born here."

"So you've never seen the sel or the King and Queen?" cried Jura.

"No, I suppose I was lucky to be born here from what I've heard about below."

"Was Octrus born here too?" asked Jura.

"Octrus?" Octalma paused. "No, no, he wasn't." Octalma's mind seemed to wander off momentarily. "Few are, in fact. No, Octrus is living a constant struggle. You can probably see it in his eyes." She paused again and Jura noticed two of her tentacles starting to wrap around each other as her mind focused on what she was about to say. "Lord Skumble has a hold on him," she continued. "And he can't seem to shake it off."

Suddenly Jura felt a wave of concern flow over her. Octrus looked so wise to her and if he could not resist Lord Skumble's dark force, however would she stand a chance? "Appearances can be deceptive," said Octalma, sensing her fear. We can never be certain which way anyone is going to go here. Octrus may look intelligent and indeed he is but really that has little to do with this. We must make choices and even the most intelligent amongst us can make the wrong ones."

"But surely if Octrus is so intelligent he can make better choices?" said Jura feeling a little confused.

"That would make sense, wouldn't it?" replied Octalma, "but we are dealing with something here that works on other realms. It cannot be calculated, predicted or manipulated and it operates in a deeper part of us. A part we can feel but cannot see or touch. We can help ourselves to resist the pull but when it comes to it, the final choice happens somewhere far inside and if that place wants to connect to Lord Skumble's force, things can be very difficult."

"But Sereno said the choice is always yours even when it may appear that it is not," interrupted Jura.

"Exactly," said Octalma. "It may appear not to be because some choices can be made from somewhere so deep inside we are not even aware of them but it is still us doing the choosing."

Jura tried hard to concentrate on what Octalma was saying. "Octrus struggles with all his heart against the part of him that is being pulled towards Lord Skumble but that part wants and even needs it to some extent and that is why he must stay so focused."

Jura stared at Octalma, questions bustling impatiently around her mind. "So how do you know if you really want to resist the pull from Lord Skumble?" she asked, "how can you be sure?"

Octalma reached out another of her tentacles and squeezed Jura comfortingly with it. "You'll know," she said. "Somewhere inside you'll know."

"Well, I know already," sprang from Jura's mouth defensively. "There's no way I'm going back down to the sel and I'm still confused why anyone would find that tempting." Octalma did not attempt to explain anymore; she knew it was something Jura would learn about gradually. She could not be expected to understand everything straightaway.

Oceans Apart

Octalma left Jura to her thoughts, she knew it was necessary for her to absorb things in her own time and she'd need some space to do this. Jura's head was beginning to feel a little crowded. There were so many thoughts pushing and shoving each other; no organization amongst them. She could not decide which ones to listen to as when she tried to single one out, a thousand others demanded equal priority. Eventually, she chose to quieten them by looking for the octopi. They would provide her with the distraction she needed. She swam over to Octalma quietly so as not to disturb a sleeping Octrus. "Do you know where the octopi are?" she whispered. Octalma had already busied herself by mending a hole that she had found in the wall. She was twisting a reed round and round and pulling it tight until the edges of the hole joined once again. She took her eyes off the task for a moment and glanced around her.

"I suppose they're still out swimming," she said, "they'll probably be back soon." Jura turned to the door expectantly. "Do you know which way they went?" she asked. She needed a distraction now; patience was not something present in her mind at this moment.

"Probably their usual," said Octalma. "Turn left out the door and keep going. You'll see them before long, they've got plenty of friends over there. In fact, when you find them could you tell them I could do with some help with this mysterious hole." Octalma seemed to be getting a little irritated as she mused over the cause of it and Jura took this as her cue to leave.

Oceans Apart

Off she swam through the reed curtain. She had become so used to her tail being held together by a reed it almost felt like part of her now. She did not stop to question her ability to swim whilst it was there. She kept it on at all times even when she was sleeping and because of this it no longer felt uncomfortable. Jura flicked her tail and off she went; alone for the first time in this part of the ocean. It felt strange to be swimming where she wanted to go rather than where someone else had in mind. She kept expecting to be told where to go and then remembering that she was the one that made those choices now, not Engano, not Sereno, no one but her.

As she swam away from Octalma's house she was very aware of the distance she was putting between her and it. She was also careful not to take any left or right turns. Octalma had said to continue straight on so that's what she must do. She must keep her wits about her. Her eyes were focused directly ahead of her, scanning the water for any sign of the octopi. Many fish passed her and Jura was pleased she now understood the looks of deep concentration. It stopped her from thinking they were being rude and feeling intimidated by them. It was a little strange nonetheless. The fish here that she had seen swimming about certainly did not give off approachable signals. Perhaps she looked like that too. "You'll see them before long," Octalma's voice echoed in her head. How long is long? she mused. Long for her would probably be very different to Octalma. Octalma's tentacles were long to Jura but to Octalma, merely part of her body. She concluded that she would carry on until Octalma's idea of long was revealed to her.

She passed a few other torn-tails swimming with their tails tied together. It was good to see she wasn't the only one being held together by a thread. They were, however, all being guided by shrimps and seeing the other shrimps sent a pang through her gills. It was not pleasant to see reminders of Sereno, especially knowing where she was now. She hoped with all her might that she would be safe and shuddered as she remembered the oppressive atmosphere in the sel. Fortunately, before she had a chance to focus too deeply on these images she caught a glimpse of a little octopus, which brought her mind back on track. She didn't realize that she had been heading in a dangerous direction.

With her mind on the octopus, Jura propelled herself a little faster. She had presumed it was either Octi or Octula. Perhaps they were playing hide and seek. As she drew closer to the octopus it soon became crystal clear that not only was there definitely only one octopus but it was also neither Octi nor Octula. This sudden realisation startled her. On seeing this octopus, she had changed direction, forgetting momentarily her plan to keep a close eye on her route so as not to lose her way. It was probably a friend of the octopi and would know where they were, she thought to herself as she approached him. "Excuse me," she said politely, "you wouldn't happen to know where I could find Octi or Octula, would you?"

The octopus lifted his dark blue eyes slowly upwards until they met Jura's. She suddenly felt a shudder of unease vibrate through her. Jura got the feeling she had interrupted this octopus when she shouldn't have. Why was it looking at her like that? What had she done wrong? Maybe she should just swim away now while she still could. Just as she was considering her options the octopus answered: "Why do you want them?" Jura's mind lurched; she had not expected to be questioned. What should she say? Purely out of habit she started desperately trying to work out what the octopus wanted to hear. Is he their friend? Perhaps an enemy. She looked deeply into his eyes hoping to catch answers to flying questions. "Well?" continued the octopus, "it's not a hard question." Jura nodded nervously. She began to panic. A million responses swirled through her, but none seemed appropriate. She did not know what was appropriate in this situation although she had spent so much time practising it in the sel. She mustn't say the wrong thing, she mustn't, she mustn't. The longer she dithered the more strangely the octopus seemed to be looking at her which, in turn, heightened her dithering. She was sending herself spiralling off and was getting dangerously close to connecting to Lord Skumble's force when fortunately the octopus helped her out. "You're from the sel, aren't you?" he said, and relieved that the silence had been broken, Jura answered, "how do you know?"

"I was asking you a straightforward question and was looking for a straightforward answer," replied the octopus.

"Well," said Jura a little nervously, "I didn't know what answer you wanted."

"How about the right one?" replied the octopus, softly.

Jura cast her eyes downwards, feeling a little ashamed. "I couldn't decide what that was," she answered quietly, feeling confused at her own confusion.

"My god, they do complicate matters down there, don't they?" continued the octopus, rubbing two of his tentacles together in despair. Jura had become so used to twisting her responses that now even the simplest of questions became a nightmare to unravel. "It's a dangerous habit you've got there," said the octopus with a serious tone "and it's not how we work here. Here you must learn to say what you really mean."

Jura's scales began to feel tight around her. The sel had changed her more than she had realized and she was beginning to see that she no longer knew what she really meant. Her responses had become based on lies, twists and on trying to please other fish and now what she actually wanted to say no longer existed in her head. Where had it gone to?

"I don't know what to say… I don't know," she shouted suddenly and she turned and swam away from the octopus, the water swallowing her tears as she swam. She swam further and further, eyes blurred, losing all sense of direction. Eventually, she found a quiet area with no sign of anyone else. A suitable thinking spot; a suitable crying spot. Although she was not entirely sure why, she had an overwhelming desire to cry. She felt confused by her situation here. She wanted Sereno to come back. She wanted to understand things that she should have been able to but couldn't. She wanted security from something or someone but everything felt strange and unfamiliar and for a moment, if only to grasp on to a thread of familiarity, her mind was drawn back to the sel. Engano, she saw his face again as he was when she had trusted him. Her loyal menfish, her tail. She started to long for that tail once more, that someone to be with her wherever she went. In a moment of destructive indulgence she had drawn Engano to her. She had succumbed to the dark temptation that she knew was wrong but somehow could not find it in her to resist. A soft warmth flowed through her as her eyes met Engano's. Green bubbles trickled towards her. He smiled the smile she was longing for and she drifted dangerously towards losing all self-control. Her eyes started to blur, her mind flickered. She could feel her pearl had not only left her but was drifting towards Engano. For that moment she wanted him to have it. She was hovering on the borderline, a force whose strength she did not understand was drawing her towards him. She craved familiarity like she had craved freedom in the sel. She began to lose the awareness that she was the one making this choice. She had initiated it but now it was operating with a potency of its own, or so it seemed, anyway.

As her pearl was about to reach Engano, his eyes focused hungrily on it. Jura felt as if there could be no turning back. All of a sudden, she was jolted back to her senses by a stabbing sensation in her fin. She was so far gone she tried desperately to ignore it but the stabbing persisted harder and harder until she was forced to return to herself. The warmth of temptation flooded out of her and as she focused her eyes once more she saw that a starfish was knocking into her repeatedly. What on earth was it doing? She felt a flash of anger towards this sharp fish that had so rudely pulled her away from the familiarity of the sel and back to her confusion. "Stop it!" she shouted. "What are you doing to me? Leave me alone." The starfish looked at Jura indignantly and left. "What a ridiculous creature," thought Jura, noticing her pearl had once again returned. She promptly decided to find her way back to Octalma's for the night, suddenly feeling very aware that she had been dangerously close to something she shouldn't have.

She darted off through the water, propelled by her aggravation at the starfish. "What a rude thing to do," she thought. She felt annoyed that the starfish had disappeared so quickly, not even stopping to hear what she had to say. If she saw her right now she would give her a piece of her mind. She had never been prodded like that before.

As she swam through the ocean in the direction she thought Octalma's house was in, the water felt unsettled around her. There seemed to be numerous thin currents running through it in many different directions. As the currents strengthened around Jura she was alerted to the fact that something was definitely not right. Her pearl was slipping from her once again and as before, her mind was concentrating on matters that seemed more important. She was focusing on getting herself through the currents. There was no clear path to follow. Just as she seemed to be getting somewhere, a current would tear across her path, knocking her off course and leaving her completely baffled as to where to go. Her irritation with the starfish was soon replaced by fear of the unpredictability of the currents. They seemed to spring out of the water at her, disorientating her every move. Sometimes she would be carried along by one current for a few seconds but just as she was beginning to regain a sense of stability she would question whether she had chosen the right direction. The moment this uncertainty entered her head she would be swept away from her current and thrown into the path of another. Her pearl was being churned around in the water. She caught glimpses of its light as it flashed through the criss-cross of currents but she had no desire to catch it. It would have been impossible, she told herself. It was moving far too fast to even attempt to bring it back to her.

Jura fought the currents with all her might, hating them with a passion. She must keep going in one direction. She flapped her aching tail frantically. Her eyes darted to and fro, desperately looking for a way out. She tried to work out which current was the strongest so she could stick to it but each time she thought she had found it, it was never the case. Occasionally, she saw another fish shooting past her on one of the currents. They seemed to be sticking to one current and managing not to be diverted by the many other ones. She wanted to watch them and see how they were doing this but there simply wasn't time. Her pearl leapt and sprung about her. She did not want it if this was how it was going to be – running away from her whenever she was in a bad situation. She needed to master the currents and its presence was a hindrance to her. She must stop the turmoil in the water – force it to let her go. Of course, a small fish in a ferocious sea cannot force tranquillity so this mentality stressed both Jura and the ocean further still.

As the currents increased their force, Jura began to have flashbacks of her escape from the sel. Was this also Lord Skumble's doing? Was he here? Perhaps he could see her. Maybe he had set this trap for her to take her pearl and her. If not then who was out to get her here? Perhaps this place was worse than the sel. Maybe she had made a fatal mistake by listening to Sereno. Maybe here she was heading for an even worse fate than the one the sel had for her. At least there, decisions were made for you. Her mind had fragmented from the pressure of the currents. Parts of it were being pulled down each vein in the water and it felt like she had nothing left to help her decide what to do. She felt like a lost, empty shell being swept away with the ocean's currents and having no say in where it took her.

There came a point where she had to admit defeat. Either she or the water had to surrender and it was showing no sign of doing any such thing. She stopped trying to control the ocean and allowed it to take her. At that moment there was no longer a fight to be had. Jura's pearl drifted back from the currents and immediately the water settled. It no longer seemed to want her life. She was handing herself over to it and now it had changed its mood entirely. Drained from eyes to tail she hovered in the water, shaken into a state of numb shock. How could the water have changed so abruptly? Had it really happened? Sapped of all energy, her eyes closed and sleep surrounded her like a warm blanket as she lay cradled and supported by the sea.

CHAPTER 11

A golden truth

She awoke outside Octalma's house and wondered briefly if she had dreamt the whole ordeal. How on earth did she manage to get back there? She drifted in through the reed curtain to find the octopi playing, Octrus thinking and Octalma making something from a ball of reeds. On seeing her, Octalma looked up. "Good swim?" she asked casually. "The octopi came back shortly after you left, they were so eager to play with you. I told them you'd probably gone off exploring." Jura did not know what to say. Everything seemed to be operating as normal. Her experience earlier had been so intense and overwhelming she expected every other creature in the ocean to be aware of it. She expected them to want to know how it felt and to listen with intrigue as she told of her near-death experience, but to everyone else life was continuing as usual. She needed to talk to Octalma about it but was a little worried about the response she would get. What if she thought she was mad and threw her out of the house? Although Octalma had never shown any signs of behaving like that, Jura did feel quite ashamed of her experience.

Jura sat in deep thought. Octalma and Octrus sensed something was not right and were fairly sure it was to do with the transition from the sel to here but didn't know exactly what. It was different for every sea creature.

Jura wanted an explanation or at least someone to talk to. She turned to Octalma and her look showed that she needed a chat. Octalma beckoned to Jura with a long tentacle and she floated over. Jura's ordeal was catching up with her again and as she recalled it she began to feel frightened.

Octalma pointed a tentacle towards the far wall of her house and an entrance appeared just big enough for them both to fit through. Jura had no idea their house contained any other rooms. "We're building a couple more as well," said Octalma excitedly. "With the octopi growing up, we just need more space." As they entered the room, Jura immediately felt more relaxed. It seemed to glow; it had a warmth to it that felt reassuring.

"What's this room for?" asked Jura.

"We haven't had it for long, to be honest," said Octalma, "but so far Octrus has taken to it. He says it has a good effect on him; that it helps him to stay here and avoid unwanted pulls, if you know what I mean." Jura did, more than Octalma knew.

"Strange things are happening to me," she told Octalma. "I think Lord Skumble is setting traps for me." Octalma looked at Jura knowingly but said nothing. Both of them waited in silence, feeling a concern that could not be fully expressed. "I think he's changing the water again like he did on my way here," Jura continued a little nervously.

Octalma listened curiously. "The pearl," she said, "how are you finding it?"

Jura felt ashamed suddenly. "Whenever anything happens it leaves me," she replied. "It disappears, I can't see the point in even having it. When it's there I don't notice it and when a bad situation arises, it no longer wants to be with me. It wriggles away and makes each situation even worse. Maybe I should just get rid of it." Even as she spoke the words she felt embarrassed to be saying them.

Octalma looked at her seriously. "I hate to be the one to break this to you but you can't just get rid of it, it's yours to look after."

"But Sereno said I had to protect it because Lord Skumble may try to steal it," said Jura. "Exactly," said Octalma "and I presume she also warned you of the consequences of such an occurrence."

Jura was silenced by her thoughts. "But can't I just get rid of it before he has a chance to get it and then he won't need to pull me down?" she asked.

"That's not how it works, I'm afraid," replied Octalma. "It's yours and providing you keep it with you and don't allow it to escape when you feel it trying to, you will have nothing to worry about. Lord Skumble will not have a chance."

"Why doesn't it decide to leave me when I can focus all my attention on it?" asked Jura. "It always disappears when my mind is elsewhere."

Octalma could see Jura's struggle and wished it was as easy as that but unfortunately they both knew it wasn't. "All I can say to you," she said, "is to keep your mind focused on your pearl whatever else is happening around you and you will be protected." Jura found it hard to listen to Octalma's advice. Her mind was still where she had just been.

"The water just turned by itself. It was horrible, so horrible I thought I was going to die," she cried. The recollection of her experience was starting to stir her up once again. "He wants me, Octalma and I'm scared he's going to keep going until he's got me." Jura felt like she was opening up to Octalma more than she had planned but she desperately needed to tell someone. "I don't know how I can stop him. I have to do something though. I have to teach him that he can't treat me like this. Yes, he must be taught."

Octalma said nothing. She had said all she could and it was Jura's choice whether she wanted to listen or not.

Having told Octalma what had happened, Jura focused on Lord Skumble. "How dare he?" she thought and began to imagine building up a force of like-minded fish and driving him out of the ocean altogether. She imagined returning to the sel with an army of fish and destroying it entirely. They would kill any fish who opposed them and set free the ones who sided with them. Then they would bring Lord Skumble up and torture him slowly until he apologized and then they'd kill him anyway.

Octalma could see that Jura's mind had gone off somewhere by the way her eyes were moving back and forth. She was quite used to this sort of reaction. So many fish had done the same thing. They would want to talk to her but at the same time would not. They would want advice but be unwilling to hear it and in the end they would create their own explanations for the things that were happening to them anyway.

Jura had chosen to forget what had really happened with the currents and with the events prior to them. She wasn't taking responsibility for anything that had happened and refused to see the relevance of a small pearl in all of this. She was so caught up in her vengeful plots that she didn't even notice Octalma leaving the room. Jura's hatred for Lord Skumble spread through her like a disease. She felt disgusted at how she had been treated and her need to see him suffer was increasing by the second. Her eyes were filling with images of destruction, of exterminating this creature who was making her life so difficult. She would have to search for enough sea creatures who were willing to join her on her mission and ensure that they were all committed to the task. How would she find these fish? She would have to spread the word.

She writhed around, her mind absorbed with matters of life and death. When at last she could contain herself no more she burst out of the door. Octalma, Octrus and the octopi jumped from the sudden eruption into the room. Their eyes followed her out of the house. While the octopi giggled at Jura's manic exit, Octalma and Octrus had more serious expressions.

The moment Jura had left the house she started to scan the area avidly for fish that would join her. "I'll get some of those long ones and the flat ones too," she thought. She darted off through the water, searching for any suitable candidates for the job. But there were none to be seen anywhere. She powered through the water, propelled by the images she had created of Lord Skumble's torture but there was not a fish in sight. She became more and more manic until her heart leapt as she spotted something coming towards her. Was it a fish? Perhaps the first to join her. As the shape drew closer it soon became clear that this was not a fish or even any sea creature at all. It was small, green and vaguely familiar. It was still too far away to identify but its presence was threatening her. As she was focused so intently on this small green object, she didn't notice that there were more following behind. She suddenly felt that someone was watching her and flicked herself around only to see more of these green objects coming from the opposite direction. As they came close enough for her to see them properly she suddenly realized what they were. They were green bubbles. The same green that Engano produced. Shocked at the amount that had crept up behind her she swung herself to the left and then quickly to the right. They were closing in on her from all angles. As they popped they clouded the water with their murky green contents, making it difficult to see. "It's Lord Skumble again," shouted a voice inside her head. "He'll try anything. Well, it's not going to work," she told herself. "I know what you're up to," she shouted into the bubble-filled water but her voice was swallowed up by the green soup that hovered in the water like a putrid fog. "Try all you like," she shouted, "but I will conquer you in the end." The more she worked herself up in her hatred for him, the more the bubbles thickened until she was completely blinded.

Not only could Jura not see but it was becoming harder and harder to breathe as well. She shouted into the thickening water, desperately trying to summon any fish that could hear her. Surely other fish must understand her predicament with Lord Skumble and want to help? Surely they too would want to conquer him and free all the fish living in the sel? She shouted as loudly as she could but the bubbles soaked up her words like a giant sponge. As they continued to multiply, she was forced into silence. She could see nothing, say nothing, hear nothing, smell nothing and feel nothing but thick, green bubbles. Her anger at Lord Skumble was forced to subside as concern for her own safety took over. Panic spread through her like an electric current. There was no way out. He had got there first. His army of green bubbles had come prepared and she was alone with no backup. Her fantasies of bringing him to justice melted away from her. She could never hope to defeat one so quick and clever. Her thoughts were suddenly disrupted by the fact that her pearl had gone. She had not even been aware of it leaving her. Sereno's words echoed through her mind: "As long as it is with you, you can come to no harm. Hand it over and trouble will undoubtedly arise." For the first time since she had been given her pearl she remembered the unique protection of it. This recollection awoke something inside her and she knew she must retrieve it. She had no idea which direction it had gone in. In this murky green expanse there was no direction.

Her eyes widened and her vision began to sharpen as the importance of finding her pearl hit her. She had to believe in it; there was no time for indecision or disbelief. She focused on breathing and seeing and after a little while the bubbles gently began to thin out, creating little pockets between them. Her mind kept trying to wander but she pulled it back and concentrated with all her might. She pictured her pearl in her mind and as she did so she felt herself relax. The bubbles slowly drifted away from her and as they did, a dull twinkle suddenly caught her eye. Was that her pearl trapped inside one of the bubbles? She approached it cautiously and then darted back in shock. It couldn't be true. Her eyes must be deceiving her. Disbelievingly, she dared to take a second look. Her eyes were not playing tricks on her. Lord Skumble was there. He was grinning at her through a green blur, his red eyes piercing the haze.

The sight of him made her feel sick. Part of her wanted to turn and swim for her life, the other part was desperate to attack him. She felt so torn that she stayed absolutely still. Lord Skumble's voice vibrated through the bubble towards her. "Straying from the sel is never a good idea," he said patronizingly. "What did you think you were hoping to gain by betraying me?" Jura did not answer. He continued: "I suppose that shrimp friend of yours failed to tell you that I always win." His eyes seemed to light up. "You have no chance of a life out of the sel. Face it, Jura, you're fully trained now. Trained to live in the real world, not this make-believe world of no-hopers. Our world. We need you Jura, but most of all, you need us. You're speaking our language now and we understand each other. No one here speaks your language or ever will; you'll be an outcast. They'll pretend you're one of them but you never will be. You collected your shells, Jura, and that is proof that you are one of us. Your life has been set up for you in the sel and you don't even need to think about it. Okay, so maybe we didn't exactly tell you the truth about the shells but you'd never have learnt what you did if we had. It was all done for your own good and leaving when your life was just about to begin is," he looked down and wiped a tear from his eye with a claw. "Well, it's such a waste." He glanced up at Jura to monitor her reaction. She didn't reveal a thing. "We both know you're an intelligent fish and we also both know that I have your pearl here. At the very least you owe me that." Jura's eyes widened involuntarily and he noted her reaction.

    Jura was speechless; she knew she was dealing with a highly unpredictable creature and must act wisely. "I'll tell you what," Lord Skumble's voice seeped through the water. "I'll take this back down to the sel while you decide what you want to do." With that, a claw reached eagerly around the bubble containing Jura's pearl and he pushed it out in front of him. Then he shot around behind Jura and in a split second had snipped off the reed that was around her tail. He swung back to face her and said, "All I'm asking is for you to realize your error and come back to the place you belong. Stay here and stay forever a torn-tail, come with me and the moment we reach the sel, you'll be given back your tail. Life without your tail or pearl is all very well, Jura, if that's the kind of life you want but it's not going to be much fun. You'll be stuck, stuck forever relying on a piece of reed to hold you together in a place where you'll never be understood."

Jura's eyes filled with hatred. It felt like her heart had a hand wrapped around it and was squeezing it tighter and tighter. "Of course your shrimp friend has come to her senses, not before time I might add, but they all do in the end."

"What?" cried Jura, unable to conceal her feelings any more.

Lord Skumble smirked. "The shrimp, the traitor that took you away from me, she's finally seen that her work is pointless. She's joined us. She asked me to apologize to you for taking you from the place you belong. She said if you go back down she'll explain."

Jura's eyes darted from side to side. "It's not true, Sereno wouldn't, you're making it up, just leave me. I'm staying here, leave me alone," she cried.

Lord Skumble pushed the bubble containing her pearl out ahead of him. "Very well," he said, "do as you will but remember what I've told you, Jura. The door is always open." He winked at her, lifted his claws and gradually began to descend through the water.

Jura's eyes were glued to her pearl as it disappeared. She had no choice but to stay where she was. Her tail had been disabled; she couldn't have followed even if she wanted to. Sereno came into her mind. What if what Lord Skumble had said was true? Did that mean that everything Sereno had told her was no longer true? If Sereno had gone against all she had said, where did that leave her? All she had said about change, about the danger of the sel. No, there was no way that could have happened. With or without Sereno, Jura had to decide wisely. It was up to her now, her alone. There was no one here to tell her what was right or wrong. Her only option was to do what she felt was right. Physically, she was in no state to move but mentally she knew there were always choices. Whatever Sereno had decided to do with her life was up to her but she remembered what she had told her and as Jura watched Lord Skumble sink back down to the sel she knew that could no longer be an option for her. If what he said about her being an outcast was true then she would live with it but she could not return to that polluted water where even breathing was a struggle. There was no way she could be another torn-tail's menfish. She could not deceive another fish like that, something inside her just would not let her. She envisaged her life if she followed Lord Skumble. The only way to achieve anything in the sel was to go against everything she instinctively felt to be right. She had been forced to do that for too long and even if it meant having a torn tail for the rest of her life, she knew that she must stay and learn once again to live in a way that worked for her and not against her.

A sudden feeling of clarity spread through her like a wave of warm water. A feeling of knowingness, a powerful awareness of what was right for her. As this happened, her senses sharpened once again. She blinked as suddenly her pearl, which Lord Skumble had taken too far away from her for her to see, was now clearly in sight. Something fluttered in her heart as she realised that both the pearl and Lord Skumble had stopped abruptly in their tracks. She could see him but he did not seem to be able to see her. What was happening? Lord Skumble was clawing frantically at the bubble her pearl was in. His eyes had ignited with anger and his mouth looked distorted. Jura's mouth fell open as she saw Lord Skumble battling with the pearl angrily as it tried to move back towards her.

As Jura watched, the warmth inside her expanded to include hope too. As this feeling spread through her, the bubble jolted out of Lord Skumble's claws and he desperately launched after it. Seeing the determination in his eyes gave Jura a jolt of fear and with that, Lord Skumble's claw curled around the bubble once again. He drew it towards him, a look of dark satisfaction spreading across his face. Her pearl was not objecting to being held by him this time. He paused briefly, looking relieved by the change then continued drawing it back down. Jura watched blankly as her pearl started to sink once more, as if it was someone else's pearl that was being taken to the sel. As its twinkle began to fade into the distance, Jura closed her eyes. Again a lightness and warmth returned to her as she reminded herself that she had a choice. Lord Skumble was not capable of anything so long as she chose to be free of him. She found herself thinking about all she had left in the sel and how different this place was. She thought of Octalma, the octopi, the clearer water, the food. She knew she was making the right decision. "Whatever happened to you in the sel will not repeat itself unless you chose to return," she remembered Sereno telling her.

The clarity that had visited her so briefly before returned with a heightened intensity. She could choose. She opened her eyes to see her pearl leave Lord Skumble's claws and shoot back through the water at a much faster speed. Jura's heart leapt as she saw it returning directly to her without a flicker of doubt. Lord Skumble was tearing after it but his attempts seemed amusing this time. He looked ridiculous; claws in chaos as they tripped over themselves in their desperation to get to the pearl. The expression on his face of utter urgency turned his mouth a funny shape and his head began to look bigger and out of proportion with his body. Suddenly, Jura could see him in a new light. He was no longer the threatening monster he liked to be seen as but more a pitiful creature whose life depended on deceiving sea creatures and stealing their pearls. She could see how terrified he was as her pearl was escaping from him and she suddenly became aware that by choosing to see Lord Skumble like this, he no longer had power over her or her pearl.

All of a sudden, he propelled himself forward

in a final convulsion of desperation and he tore at the bubble containing Jura's pearl. As his pincer touched it, the bubble burst and a cloud of green grime exploded in his face, blinding him. This supposedly dangerous creature was reduced to a spluttering wreck as he choked on his own poison. Jura's pearl whooshed towards her and as it neared her she felt her heart expand. She had done it; she really was capable of choosing and merely the realization of this had brought her pearl back.

As her pearl drew closer to her, Jura opened her fin but it had no intention of stopping whatsoever. Instead, it slowed down slightly and as it did so it sent an intense, tingling sensation right through Jura. When this feeling subsided, her body felt weightless and she found herself instinctively following it. It was shooting up through the water urgently. Jura knew it wasn't trying to get away from her because she knew it belonged with her.

As they raced up through the water, Jura felt overwhelmed by a feeling of freedom. She was moving so smoothly and at such speed and yet with absolutely no effort. It was almost as if she was being carried by another fish except there was a difference. She could feel it was her alone that was causing her to speed through the water so easily. She was being guided by her pearl but she was moving all by herself. How could this be? She didn't even have a… That was it, her tail – somehow it was working again. She definitely had no reed holding it together as Lord Skumble had taken that yet it was working as good as new. She was no longer a torn-tail. Her eyes filled with tears of joy as this realization spread through her. She swished her tail in exaggerated waves and sure enough, not a drop of water slipped through it. Her speed just increased further still. She experimented with it, swishing it fast and then slow, swaying it in wide strokes and then switching to tiny little movements. She even made patterns in the water with it. She realized that small circular rotations increased her speed and large ones slowed her down but stabilized her. She stretched herself out as far as she could, making her body long and thin. As she did this she cut through the water like a knife. Then she puffed herself out and concentrated on feeling round; her speed decreased and she began to float upwards like an inflated balloon.

Completely absorbed in her different swimming styles, she had not noticed how far up they had ventured. She took her mind from her tail for a moment and looked where she was. Her pearl had slowed down, allowing her to see what was around her. The water was crystal clear and so fresh. Her body felt more alive immediately as she breathed in this clean water.

Silver fish glided through the water, their eyes sparkling like jewels. Shafts of sunlight sliced through the surface of the sea and reflected off their scales. Multicoloured beams of light bounced back through the water, causing Jura's pearl to glow like she'd never seen it before. The sun's heat had gently warmed the water to a temperature that soothed Jura so much she finally understood what it felt to be truly relaxed. There was so much space all around her and the water was so clear that, for the first time in her life she could actually see what her eyes were capable of. She could literally see for miles. In the distance she could see large creatures lunging themselves out of the water and diving back under again. The joy this game gave them could be felt for miles around them as it rippled through the water. Jura had no idea what these creatures were but knew she wanted to join in the fun.

Close by, a shoal of turquoise and yellow fish were swimming in a way she had never seen before. It was as if they were dancing to music only they could hear. Their fins moved in synchrony to a rhythm that was continually changing and somehow they all just knew when to change direction without needing to communicate with each other. Jura watched in awe as the pattern they swam in switched and changed with the ease of a beating heart. She wondered how they all knew with such precision the movements of the hundreds of other fish in the shoal and it delighted her to watch them.

Jura's new surroundings were almost hypnotic to her. The sense of calm that vibrated through the water here was so unlike anything she had ever experienced before. The change in atmosphere from the sel to where Octalma lived was one thing but this place was magical. Jura felt peaceful but her pearl was like an excited child eager to experience everything it could feel around it. As she became deeply absorbed in her new surroundings she was shocked to see something floating towards her. It wasn't a fish or any kind of sea creature. It was small and round and its form was familiar but it was a colour she had never seen before.

Oceans Apart

It was a golden bubble. Despite her experience with bubbles in the past, she was surprisingly unthreatened by this one. She knew instinctively it was nothing to be scared of. As it floated towards her, she wondered what had produced this golden bubble. No sooner had the thought crossed her mind than the bubble bearer glided into view.

Her initial thought was one of confusion. What on earth was this creature? She wasn't a fish or a lobster or a crab or a shrimp or an eel or an octopus. She was a strange sort of elongated shape with a curly tail and a slightly pointy face with eager, kind eyes. She was golden in colour and shone as brightly as the sun itself. Jura found herself moving towards this bizarre creature, fascinated. As the space between them decreased, a cluster of golden bubbles danced towards Jura. The seahorse opened her mouth. "I'm so pleased to see you, Jura," she said with a voice so comforting and soothing Jura wanted to wrap herself up in it.

"How do you know my name?" Jura replied, knowing they hadn't met before.

"Come." The seahorse beckoned with its tail and bobbed off slowly in the direction of the dolphins. Jura followed obediently, feeling intrigued by this golden creature that seemed to know her.

They swam along beside each other for a minute or so before the seahorse spoke. "Firstly," she said, "I would like to congratulate you for being here."

Jura felt puzzled. "I just seemed to end up here," she replied, "I didn't do anything."

"Now that, I'm afraid, is where I will have to

step in and correct you," said the seahorse, "you, my dear Jura, have done the most extraordinary amount."

"But," interrupted Jura, and then stopped herself, as she realised this funny-looking creature was about to say something important.

"You are now at the point," continued the seahorse "where you are ready to hear the final explanation." Jura watched the golden bubbles as they popped, releasing tiny explosions of light like miniature stars erupting into a crystal-clear infinity. The seahorse paused and their eyes met for a brief moment before she continued. "You, my dear Jura, are responsible for everything you have experienced in your life so far. And do you know why that is?" the seahorse asked. Jura did not respond. "It is because everything you have seen in your life you attracted because you needed to see it. Every sea creature you have ever met has not just randomly popped into your life. They have all been there for a reason. From the day you were born you knew things weren't right, did you not?" Jura could hardly disagree with that. "Well, you attracted the sel and all its unsavoury inhabitants into your life in order to feel just how wrong things were. The bubbles you learnt lessons in were coloured by the nature of each one. The black bubble was about hatred, revenge and malice, the green represented deceit and the red was a lesson in anger. In a sense, you imprisoned yourself, Jura. All the deceit you experienced was something you had to learn about." Jura's fin twitched; she felt a little uncomfortable hearing these words. "But you also chose to escape from the sel and brought Sereno into your life to make this possible."

"Hang on," cried Jura, "you're saying I wanted to live in the sel and I wanted to learn all those horrible lessons? How can you say that – all I ever wanted was a peaceful life."

The seahorse looked at Jura kindly. "I know it seemed like that and in the end that is what you chose but you did choose to live in the sel too. You're not alone, Jura. Every fish attracts different friends and enemies into their lives depending on what it is they need to learn. Some will be drawn to the sel or something similar and will never escape from it; others will stay under the rule of the King and Queen and never question a thing. The occasional fish will find its way here without creating any major obstacles. It is up to each individual fish how many obstacles it creates for itself. Some never believe it is possible to live in a place like this where you can actually feel the warmth from the sun, so they attract everything that reinforces that belief. You are all living in the same sea but the lives you are living are oceans apart."

Jura had remembered Sereno talking about the difficulties some fish had with resisting the pull from Lord Skumble, she guessed this was what the seahorse was talking about.

"But why, why are we all doing this? Wouldn't it be better if you went down there and explained to all the fish what they were doing? If you know all this, how can you just stay here and let all those fish live that way?"

"Sounds so simple, doesn't it?" replied the

seahorse, "but that is impossible. It is the law of the ocean. All fish are free to choose where and how they want to live and it is certainly not for me or anyone else to interfere. If they chose to find their way up here they are ready to hear the truth. Telling them in another place would be going against the law of the ocean and they would not hear what I was saying anyway.

"So could you see me then?" asked Jura.

"Not exactly," continued the seahorse, "but I can feel the goings on in the ocean and can focus on any one fish in particular to find out what's happening."

Jura felt puzzled. "This is completely normal," the seahorse continued. "You have not been doing anything out of the ordinary. Every fish is always choosing even when it appears that they are not. Sereno and Octalma explained a bit about choice to you, didn't they?" Jura thought to the conversation she'd had with Sereno soon after her escape from the sel. The seahorse continued: "Sereno also told you about the importance of keeping your pearl with you. Every stage in your life has been chosen by you. You have made your way here and so will others that want to."

Hearing this made Jura feel embarrassed. It seemed ridiculous to have lived in the sel when a place like this was here all along. The choices she had made in the past were not something she was proud of. What an obstacle course she had set up for herself in order to get here. She had learned a lot along the way, though and now she had an even greater understanding of her place in the ocean. Whatever it took to get her here, at least she now knew the answer to the question she had asked: There certainly is more food higher up in the ocean.

The End

Printed in Great Britain
by Amazon.co.uk, Ltd.,
Marston Gate.